THE DECAPITATED CHICKEN
and Other Stories

Other Texas Pan American paperbacks

The Texas Pan American Series

The Decapitated Chicken

and Other Stories by Horacio Quiroga

Selected & translated by Margaret Sayers Peden

Introduction by George D. Schade

Illustrations by Ed Lindlof

University of Texas Press   Austin

The Texas Pan American Series is published
with the assistance of a revolving publication fund
established by the Pan American Sulphur Company.

Library of Congress Cataloging in Publication Data

Quiroga, Horacio, 1879–1937.
The decapitated chicken, and other stories.

(The Texas Pan American series)
CONTENTS: The feather pillow.—Sunstroke.—
The pursued. [etc.]
I. Title.
PZ3.Q5De10   [PQ8519.Q5]   75-40167
ISBN 0-292-71541-2 pbk.

Contents

Introduction

A new edition of Horacio Quiroga stories—in this case, the first
selective translation into English ranging over his complete work
—reminds us of a superb writer and offers a pretext for talking
about him. Of course, the round dozen stories which make up this
volume can speak for themselves, and many translations appear
unescorted by an introduction; nonetheless, readers who are not
acquainted with Quiroga may wish to learn something further
about this author, generally regarded by the critics as a classic
and one of the finest short-story writers Latin America has produced. Surveying his work afresh, we find that this favorable
verdict still holds true and that his achievement continues to be
admirable. Quiroga stands apart from the bulk of his contem-
poraries in Spanish American literature and head and shoulders
above most of them.

Certain thematic designs run through Quiroga's life and also
through his stories. He was born the last day of the year 1878 in
El Salto, Uruguay, and died by his own hand in February, 1937,
in Buenos Aires, Argentina. The fifty-eight–year span of his lifetime was crammed with adventure, hazardous enterprise, and
recurrent tragedy and violence, particularly suicide. When he
was a babe in arms, his father was accidentally killed when a shotgun went off on a family outing. Later his stepfather, desperately
ill and of whom Horacio was fond, shot himself, and the young
Quiroga, seventeen at the time, was the first to come upon the
grisly scene. In 1902 Quiroga accidentally shot and killed, with
a pistol, one of his best friends and literary companions. In 1915
his first wife, unable to endure the hardships of life in the jungle
of Misiones where Quiroga insisted on living, committed suicide
by taking a fatal dose of poison, leaving the widower with two
small children to raise. Finally, Quiroga himself took cyanide to

end his own life when he realized he was suffering from an incurable cancer.

His love affairs and marriages were also turbulent. He married twice, both times very young women; his second wife, a friend of his daughter, was nearly thirty years his junior. The first marriage ended with his wife's suicide; the second, in separation. This singular amount of violence marring the writer's personal life cannot be overly stressed, for it explains a great deal about his obsession with death, which is so marked in his work.

Quiroga's zest for adventure and the magnetic attraction the jungle hinterland of northern Argentina held for him are also biographical details that have great impact on his work. His first trip to the province of Misiones occurred in 1903, when he accompanied his friend and fellow writer Leopoldo Lugones as photographer on an expedition to study the Jesuit ruins there. Next came a trip to the Chaco to plant cotton, where he built his own hut and had his first pioneering experience. In 1906 he bought some land in San Ignacio, Misiones, and from that date on divided his time between the hinterland and Buenos Aires. He tried various experiments in Misiones, such as the making of charcoal and the distillation of an orange liqueur. These endeavors ended in failure but provided him with good material for his stories, as did his myriad other activities there, like constructing his bungalow, furniture, and boats and hunting and studying the wildlife of the region.

In his teens Quiroga began writing under the aegis of the Modernist movement, which dominated the Spanish American literary scene at the turn of the century. Soon, however, he reacted against the decadent and highly artificial mode of his first book, *Los arrecifes de coral* (Coral reefs, published 1901), which contained Modernist poems, prose pieces, and stories, and turned to writing tales firmly rooted in reality, though they often emphasized the bizarre or the monstrous.

Commentators have tended to discount the significance or merit of some of Quiroga's early works, such as the longish story "The Pursued." Recently this tale has received more favorable critical attention. Our translator, who has made an excellent selection of Quiroga's stories that few would quarrel with, maintains that "The Pursued" is the most modern piece he wrote because of what it anticipates. It is undeniably one of Quiroga's more ambiguous and inscrutable stories, lending itself to various interpretations as it elaborates on the theme of madness.

Another early story, "The Feather Pillow," first published in 1907, is a magnificent example of his successful handling of the Gothic tale, reminiscent of Poe, whom he revered as master. The effects of horror, something mysterious and perverse pervading the atmosphere, are all there from the beginning of the story, and Quiroga skillfully, gradually readies the terrain, so that we are somewhat prepared for, though we do not anticipate, the sensational revelation at the end. But this story takes on much more meaning and subtlety when we realize that the anecdote can be interpreted on a symbolical level: the ailing Alicia suffers from hallucinations brought on by her husband's hostility and coldness, for he is the real monster.

For three decades Quiroga continued writing and publishing stories in great quantity—his total output runs over two hundred—many of them also of impressive quality. Certain collections should be singled out as high points: *Los desterrados* (The exiled, published 1926) and *Cuentos de amor, de locura, y de muerte* (Stories of love, madness, and death, published 1917). The splendid title of *Cuentos* sets forth his major themes and could properly be the heading for his entire work. Quiroga also achieved great popularity with his *Cuentos de la selva* (published 1918), translated into English as *Jungle Tales*, a volume for children of all ages, permeated with tenderness and humor and filled with whimsy. These delightful stories are peopled by talking animals and are cast in a fable mold, usually with an underlying moral.

"Anaconda," which describes a world of snakes and vipers and how they battle men and also one another, is one of Quiroga's most celebrated stories. It moves at a more leisurely pace than the typical Quiroga tale, with spun-out plot, lingering over realistic details. The characters in this ophidian world are more compelling than believable, and the animal characterization is not perhaps as striking as that of some shorter narratives like "Sunstroke." But Quiroga, the fluent inventor at work, can almost always make something interesting happen. "Anaconda" lies on the ill-defined frontier between the long story and the novella and will gainsay those who think Quiroga sacrifices everything to rapid narrative. Consequently, it loses something of the dramatic intensity of other stories, despite its original title of "A Drama in the Jungle: The Vipers' Empire." The tight-knit, tense structure we can perceive in "Drifting," "The Dead Man," and many other Quiroga stories is considerably slackened here. On the other hand, Quiroga compensates for this by offering us a story of exuberant imagination, rich in irony, with abundant satirical implications about man and his behavior. Like the *Jungle Tales*, "Anaconda" will have a special appeal for children, but, unlike the former, it is essentially directed to a mature audience.

If we examine Quiroga's stories attentively, we will find moments full of vision concerning mankind, often illuminating a whole character or situation in a flash. Quiroga has an astute awareness of the problems besetting man on every side, not only the pitfalls of savage Nature but also those pertaining to human relationships. Man is moved by greed and overweening ambition, hampered by fate, and often bound by circumstances beyond his control. Quiroga penetrates the frontiers of profound dissatisfaction and despair felt by man. His vision is clear and ruthless, and his comments on human illusions can be withering. Yet it is man's diversity that emerges in these stories, his abjectness and his heroism. Though Quiroga never palliates man's faults and weaknesses, the heroic virtues of courage, generosity, and compassion stand out in many of his stories.

All this rich and multifarious human material is shaped and patterned into story form by a master craftsman. Quiroga was very conscious of the problems involved in the technique and art of the short story, and, like Edgar Allan Poe and other masters of the genre, he wrote about them. His most famous document on technique is what he dubbed a "Manual of the Perfect Short Story Writer," a succinct decalogue filled with cogent and compelling advice. The usual warnings stressing economy of expression are here: for instance, "Don't use unnecessary adjectives"; and also those concerned with careful advance planning: "Don't start to write without knowing from the first word where you are going. In a story that comes off well, the first three lines are as important as the last three." It is easy to find apt examples of the latter dictum in Quiroga's work: "Drifting," "The Dead Man," "The Decapitated Chicken," "The Feather Pillow," and so on, to cite only from the stories translated in this collection.

The last commandment in Quiroga's decalogue to the person desiring to write perfect short stories is probably the most suggestive: "Don't think about your friends when you write or the impression your story will make. Tell the tale as if the story's only interest lay in the small surroundings of your characters, of which you might have been one. In no other way is *life* achieved in the short story." Quite rightly Quiroga emphasizes the word *life*, for it is this elusive and vital quality which lies at the core of his stories. The idea that the author or his narrator might be one of the characters is also significant, for he often was one of the characters, at least in some aspect, or felt that he was one of them.

Certainly in his best stories Quiroga practiced the economy he talks about in his manual and which is characteristic of good short-story writers. Almost every page will bear testimony to this laconic quality. It is a brevity which excludes everything redundant but nothing which is really significant. Wonderful feats of condensation are common, as in "The Dead Man," where he shows his powers in dramatic focus on a single scene, or in "Drifting," a stark story in which everything seems reduced to the essential, the indispensable. The brief opening scene of "Drifting," where a man is bitten by a venomous snake, contains the germs of all that comes afterward. The language is terse and pointed, the situation of tremendous intensity, the action straightforward and lineal. Everything moves in an unbroken line from beginning to end, like an arrow to its target, to use Quiroga's phrase referring to technique in the short story. The title, too, is particularly appropriate: while the dying protagonist literally drifts in his canoe downriver seeking aid, we see him helplessly adrift on the river of life, unable to control his fatal destiny from the moment the snake sinks its fangs into his foot.

In "Drifting," "The Son," "The Dead Man," and other stories, Quiroga plays on a life/death vibration, juxtaposing the two. While the throes of death slowly diminish the protagonist of "The Dead Man," Nature and the landscape surrounding him pulsate with life—the ordinary domestic quality of daily life he is so accustomed to—so that he cannot accept the fact of his dying. Our curiosity is kept unfalteringly alive by Quiroga's dramatic technique. At his finest moments Quiroga reaches and maintains a high degree of emotional intensity, as in the three stories cited above, which have in common their magnificent treatment of death. Quiroga flinches from none of the difficulties perhaps implicit in this theme. In his dealing with death he is natural and matter-of-fact; we find no mawkish romantic sentimentality, no glossing over of realistic attributes, and no gloating over ugly clinical details characteristic of naturalistic writers.

There is also much suggestion and implication, rather than outright telling, in Quiroga's best work. "The Dead Man" is probably the most skillful instance of this technique, but interesting examples abound throughout Quiroga's narratives. A case in point is the heartfelt story "The Son," where the protagonist father, suffering from hallucinations, imagines that his young son, who went hunting in the forest, has had a fatal accident. The father stumbles along in a frenzy, cutting his way through the thick and treacherous jungle, seeking a sign of the boy. Suddenly he stifles a cry, for he has seen something in the sky. The suggestion, confirmed later by the boy's death at the end of the story, is that the father saw a buzzard.

Dialogue does not play a heavy role in Quiroga's work. Occasionally we listen to scraps of talk, but, in the main, his stories do not move by dialogue; they are thrust along by overt action. Exceptions to this rule are "Anaconda" and some other animal tales. A stunning example of Quiroga's handling of dialogue occurs in "A Slap in the Face" toward the end of the story where the peon wreaks his terrible revenge on Korner, beating the boss into a bloody, inert pulp with his riding whip. Here Quiroga contrasts most effectively Korner's silence, symbolical of his beaten condition, with the peon's crackling commands *Levántate* ("Get up") and *Caminá* ("Get going"), the only words uttered in the latter part of this violent, sadistic scene. The word *caminá*, repeated four times at slight intervals, suggests an onomatopoeic fusion with the sound of the cracking whip, another instance of Quiroga's technical genius—language functioning to blend auditory effects with content.

Narrative interest seems to prevail over other elements which often dominate in the short story, such as the poetical, symbolical, or philosophical. And Quiroga does not have a social ax to grind. But some of the most trenchant social commentary in Spanish American fiction can be perceived in his stories, particularly those concerned with the exploitation of Misiones lumberjacks, like "Los mensú" ("The Monthly Wage Earners") and "A Slap in the Face." In these tales no preaching is involved. Quiroga is clearly on the side of the oppressed but does not express their point of view exclusively. Consequently, the reader draws his own conclusions, and the social impact is more deeply felt.

Setting, as well as narrative technique, is vitally important to Quiroga, because it is inseparable from the real, the ordinary, domestic, day-to-day experience of human existence. Quiroga's feelings are bound up in place, in his adopted corner of Argentina, Misiones province, rather than the urban centers of Buenos Aires or Montevideo, where he also lived. He is vastly attracted to the rugged jungle landscape, where the majority of his best stories take place (nine of the twelve translated here). And he makes us feel the significance of his setting, too—the symbolic strength of the rivers, especially the Paraná, and the power and hypnotic force of its snake-infested jungles. So does this dot on the map that is Misiones come throbbingly alive for us. It is not just a framework in which to set his stories but an integral part of them, of Quiroga himself, brimming over with drama and life.

In the best stories, many of which appear in this collection, action is perfectly illustrative: the stories have not only move ment but also depth. The apparent spareness allows for a greater complexity and suggestion. A fine short story should have implications which will continue to play in the reader's mind when the story is done and over, as we can attest in "The Feather Pillow," "The Dead Man," and almost all the stories included here. We are struck at the end of "A Slap in the Face" by the dual function of the river, which provides the final solution. The peon thrusts the almost lifeless, despicable Korner onto a raft where he will drift inevitably to his death, while the peon takes off in a boat in the opposite direction toward haven on the Brazilian shore. Thus the river assumes the role of justice, meting out death to the guilty and life to the accused. "Juan Darién" is probably one of the most subtle and interesting stories Quiroga ever penned. Rich in suggestions, it opens up to us a world of fantastic reality in which the protagonist is a tiger/boy. At one point in the story Quiroga has the inspector say that truth can be much stranger than fiction. Interpretations of this story will vary, but the most rewarding one may well be that of Juan Darién as a Christ-like figure.

Swift recognition for his mastery of the short story came to Quiroga fairly early in his career, and he continued to enjoy fame throughout his lifetime. In the Spanish-speaking world he is still popular today and almost universally admired, though the type of story he excelled at, in which man is pitted against Nature and rarely if ever wins out, is no longer so commonly composed in Latin America. The contemporary Argentine Julio Cortázar, a writer very unlike Quiroga but also topflight in the short-story genre, has pointed out perspicaciously Quiroga's best and most lasting qualities: he knew his trade in and out; he was universal in dimension; he subjected his themes to dramatic form, transmitting to his readers all their virtues, all their ferment, all their projection in depth; he wrote tautly and described with intensity so that the story would make its mark on the reader, nailing itself in his memory.

Quiroga's is an art that speaks to us clearly and passionately, charged with the emotion of his jungle setting. The action is usually of heroic simplicity. Quiroga does not transcribe life; he dramatizes it. His vision is fresh, intense, dramatic. He seems caught up in it, and so are we.

George D. Schade

The Quiroga stories in this book are available in several Spanish editions. In translating these stories I used the Biblioteca Rodó Series (Horacio Quiroga, *Cuentos*, Biblioteca Rodó Series, Montevideo, 1937–1945), in which the stories are located as follows:

"Sunstroke" ("La insolación," vol. 2)
"The Pursued" ("Los perseguidos," vol. 7)
"The Decapitated Chicken" ("La gallina degollada," vol. 1)
"Drifting" ("A la deriva," vol. 1)
"A Slap in the Face" ("Una bofetada," vol. 1)
"In the Middle of the Night" ("En la noche," vol. 3)
"Juan Darién" ("Juan Darién," vol. 4)
"The Dead Man" ("El hombre muerto," vol. 2)
"Anaconda" ("Anaconda," vol. 3)
"The Incense Tree Roof" ("El techo de incienso," vol. 5)
"The Son" ("El hijo," vol. 1)

I took "The Feather Pillow" ("El almohadón de pluma") from Quiroga's *Sus mejores cuentos*, with introduction and notes by John A. Crow (Mexico City: Editorial Cultura, 1943).

The Feather Pillow

Her entire honeymoon gave her hot and cold shivers. A blond, angelic, and timid young girl, the childish fancies she had dreamed about being a bride had been chilled by her husband's rough character. She loved him very much, nonetheless, although sometimes she gave a light shudder when, as they returned home through the streets together at night, she cast a furtive glance at the impressive stature of her Jordan, who had been silent for an hour. He, for his part, loved her profoundly but never let it be seen.

For three months—they had been married in April—they lived in a special kind of bliss. Doubtless she would have wished less severity in the rigorous sky of love, more expansive and less cautious tenderness, but her husband's impassive manner always restrained her.

The house in which they lived influenced her chills and shuddering to no small degree. The whiteness of the silent patio—friezes, columns, and marble statues—produced the wintry impression of an enchanted palace. Inside, the glacial brilliance of stucco, the completely bare walls, affirmed the sensation of unpleasant coldness. As one crossed from one room to another, the echo of his steps reverberated throughout the house, as if long abandonment had sensitized its resonance.

Alicia passed the autumn in this strange love nest. She had determined, however, to cast a veil over her former dreams and live like a sleeping beauty in the hostile house, trying not to think about anything until her husband arrived each evening.

It is not strange that she grew thin. She had a light attack of influenza that dragged on insidiously for days and days: after that Alicia's health never returned. Finally one afternoon she was able to go into the garden, supported on her husband's arm. She looked around listlessly. Suddenly Jordan, with deep tenderness, ran his hand very slowly over her head, and Alicia instantly burst into sobs, throwing her arms around his neck. For a long time she cried out all the fears she had kept silent, redoubling her weeping at Jordan's slightest caress. Then her sobs subsided, and she stood a long while, her face hidden in the hollow of his neck, not moving or speaking a word.

This was the last day Alicia was well enough to be up. On the following day she awakened feeling faint. Jordan's doctor examined her with minute attention, prescribing calm and absolute rest.

"I don't know," he said to Jordan at the street door. "She has a great weakness that I am unable to explain. And with no vomiting, nothing . . . if she wakes tomorrow as she did today, call me at once."

When she awakened the following day, Alicia was worse. There was a consultation. It was agreed there was an anemia of incredible progression, completely inexplicable. Alicia had no more fainting spells, but she was visibly moving toward death. The lights were lighted all day long in her bedroom, and there was complete silence. Hours went by without the slightest sound. Alicia dozed. Jordan virtually lived in the drawing room, which was also always lighted. With tireless persistence he paced ceaselessly from one end of the room to the other. The carpet swallowed his steps. At times he entered the bedroom and continued his silent pacing back and forth alongside the bed, stopping for an instant at each end to regard his wife.

Suddenly Alicia began to have hallucinations, vague images, at first seeming to float in the air, then descending to floor level. Her eyes excessively wide, she stared continuously at the carpet on either side of the head of her bed. One night she suddenly focused on one spot. Then she opened her mouth to scream, and pearls of sweat suddenly beaded her nose and lips.

"Jordan! Jordan!" she clamored, rigid with fright, still staring at the carpet.

Jordan ran to the bedroom, and, when she saw him appear, Alicia screamed with terror.

"It's I, Alicia, it's I!"

Alicia looked at him confusedly; she looked at the carpet; she looked at him once again; and after a long moment of stupefied confrontation, she regained her senses. She smiled and took her husband's hand in hers, caressing it, trembling, for half an hour.

Among her most persistent hallucinations was that of an anthropoid poised on his fingertips on the carpet, staring at her.

The doctors returned, but to no avail. They saw before them a diminishing life, a life bleeding away day by day, hour by hour, absolutely without their knowing why. During their last consultation Alicia lay in a stupor while they took her pulse, passing her inert wrist from one to another. They observed her a long time in silence and then moved into the dining room.

"Phew . . ." The discouraged chief physician shrugged his shoulders. "It is an inexplicable case. There is little we can do . . ."

"That's my last hope!" Jordan groaned. And he staggered blindly against the table.

Alicia's life was fading away in the subdelirium of anemia, a delirium which grew worse throughout the evening hours but which let up somewhat after dawn. The illness never worsened during the daytime, but each morning she awakened pale as death, almost in a swoon. It seemed only at night that her life drained out of her in new waves of blood. Always when she awakened she had the sensation of lying collapsed in the bed with a million-pound weight on top of her. Following the third day of this relapse she never left her bed again. She could scarcely move her head. She did not want her bed to be touched, not even to have her bedcovers arranged. Her crepuscular terrors advanced now in the form of monsters that dragged themselves toward the bed and laboriously climbed upon the bedspread.

Then she lost consciousness. The final two days she raved ceaselessly in a weak voice. The lights funereally illuminated the bedroom and drawing room. In the deathly silence of the house the only sound was the monotonous delirium from the bedroom and the dull echoes of Jordan's eternal pacing.

Finally, Alicia died. The servant, when she came in afterward to strip the now empty bed, stared wonderingly for a moment at the pillow.

"Sir!" she called Jordan in a low voice. "There are stains on the pillow that look like blood."

Jordan approached rapidly and bent over the pillow. Truly, on the case, on both sides of the hollow left by Alicia's head, were two small dark spots.

"They look like punctures," the servant murmured after a moment of motionless observation.

"Hold it up to the light," Jordan told her.

The servant raised the pillow but immediately dropped it and stood staring at it, livid and trembling. Without knowing why, Jordan felt the hair rise on the back of his neck.

"What is it?" he murmured in a hoarse voice.

"It's very heavy," the servant whispered, still trembling.

Jordan picked it up; it was extraordinarily heavy. He carried it out of the room, and on the dining room table he ripped open the case and the ticking with a slash. The top feathers floated away, and the servant, her mouth opened wide, gave a scream of horror and covered her face with her clenched fists: in the bottom of the pillowcase, among the feathers, slowly moving its hairy legs, was a monstrous animal, a living, viscous ball. It was so swollen one could scarcely make out its mouth.

Night after night, since Alicia had taken to her bed, this abomination had stealthily applied its mouth—its proboscis one might better say—to the girl's temples, sucking her blood. The puncture was scarcely perceptible. The daily plumping of the pillow had doubtlessly at first impeded its progress, but as soon as the girl could no longer move, the suction became vertiginous. In five days, in five nights, the monster had drained Alicia's life away.

These parasites of feathered creatures, diminutive in their habitual environment, reach enormous proportions under certain conditions. Human blood seems particularly favorable to them, and it is not rare to encounter them in feather pillows.

Sunstroke

Old, the puppy, went out the door and across the patio, walking lazily but erect. He paused at the edge of the grass, stretched in the direction of the bush; eyes half-closed, nose twitching, he sat down, tranquil. He could see before him the monotonous plains of the Chaco with its alternating bush and fields, fields and bush—its only color the cream of the dried grass and the black of the bush. Two hundred meters away, on the horizon, the bush closed in three sides of a tilled field. Toward the fourth side, on the west, the fields widened out into a valley framed in the distance by the inescapable line of the jungle.

At that early hour, in contrast to the obfuscating light of mid-day, the boundary had an air of restful clarity. There was neither a cloud in the sky nor a breath of air stirring. Beneath the calm of the silvery sky the fields exuded a tonic freshness that could bring to a pensive soul, facing the certainty of another day of dryness, melancholy thoughts of work better rewarded.

Milk, the puppy's father, in his turn crossed the patio and sat down beside Old with a lazy sigh of well-being. Both lay motionless, since it was still too early to be bothered by flies.

Old, who for a while had been staring into the bush, observed, "It's a cool morning."

Milk followed the puppy's gaze and lay staring, blinking distractedly. After a while, he said, "There are two falcons in that tree."

They glanced indifferently toward a passing ox and continued, as was their custom, to observe the things around them.

In the meantime the eastern sky began to open like a purple fan, and the horizon had now lost its early-morning preciseness. Milk crossed his front feet and felt a slight twinge of pain. Without moving, he looked at his toes, deciding finally to sniff them.

The preceding day he had extracted a thorn from his paw, and in memory of what he had suffered he generously licked the injured toe.

"Couldn't walk," he exclaimed as he finished with his paw.

Old didn't know what he was referring to. Milk added, "There's lots of thorns."

This time the pup understood, and in agreement he replied, after a long silence, "There's lots of thorns."

Both fell silent again, convinced.

The sun came out, and in the first bath of light the air filled with the brassy concert of the wild turkey's tumultuous trumpeting. The dogs, gilded in the oblique sunlight, rolled back their eyes, settling into luxury, blinking their eyes devoutly. One by one the pair was augmented by the arrival of other companions: Dick, the taciturn favorite; Prince, whose upper lip had been split by a coati, revealing his teeth; and Isondú, the only one of the dogs with a native name. Stretched out, stupified with well-being, the five fox terriers slept.

At the end of an hour they raised their heads; from the opposite side of the bizarre two-storied ranch house—the lower floor of clay and the upper of wood, with chaletlike balconies and railing—they had heard their master's footsteps descending the stairs. Mister Jones, his towel over his shoulder, paused a moment at the corner of the house and looked at the sun, already high in the sky. He was still bleary eyed and droopy lipped after his more than usually prolonged solitary evening of drinking.

As he washed, the dogs approached and, lazily wagging their tails, sniffed his boots. Like wild animals that have become tame, dogs know the least sign of their master's drunkenness. Slowly they moved away and again lay down in the sun. But soon the rising heat forced them to abandon the sunlight for the shade of the balconies.

The day advanced as had all the preceding days of the month: dry, clear, fourteen hours of calcining sun that seemed to melt the sky and in an instant split the dew-dampened earth into whitish scabs. Mister Jones went to his field, observed the preceding day's work, and returned to the house. He did no work that morning. He ate lunch and went upstairs for his siesta.

In spite of the burning sun, the peons returned about two to their hoeing, since nothing stops weeds from growing in cotton plants. The dogs followed them to the field, great aficionados of cultivation ever since the preceding winter when they had learned to challenge the falcons for the white worms turned up by the plow. Each of the dogs stretched out beneath a cotton plant, their panting accompanying the dull thuds of the hoe.

Meanwhile, it grew hotter. In the silent and sun-blinded landscape, the shimmering light wounded the eyes. The peons, mutely working the fields and swathed to their ears in kerchiefs, were struck by oven-hot blasts of air from the freshly turned earth. From time to time the dogs changed position, choosing a new plant in an attempt to find cooler shade. They stretched out full length, but often their fatigue would oblige them to sit up to facilitate breathing.

Shimmering before their eyes was a clayey hillock which no one had ever attempted to plow. There, suddenly, the puppy saw Mister Jones, sitting on a tree trunk and staring at him. Old stood up, wagging his tail. The others, too, rose to their feet, but with hair bristling.

"It's the *patrón*," exclaimed the puppy, surprised by the attitude of the others.

"No, that's not him," Dick replied.

The four dogs stood together growling quietly, their eyes glued on the figure of Mister Jones, who stood motionless, staring at them. The pup, incredulous, was about to move toward him, but Prince snarled at him, showing his teeth.

"That isn't him, that's Death."

The pup's hair rose in fright and he moved back to the group.

"Is the *patrón* dead?" he asked anxiously.

The others, without answering, broke into furious barking but maintained a fearful attitude. But now Mister Jones was dissolving in the shimmering air.

Hearing the barking, the peons had looked up but had seen

nothing. They turned their heads around to see if some horse had entered the field and then again bent over their work.

The fox terriers started back toward the house. The pup, his hair still on end, ran ahead and then dropped back with short nervous trotting steps; he had learned from the behavior of his companions that, when a thing is about to die, it first makes an appearance.

"And how do you know that what we saw wasn't the *patrón*, alive?" he asked.

"Because it wasn't him," they answered peevishly.

So it was to be Death, and with her a change of owners, misery, kicking; all this lay before them! They spent the remainder of the afternoon by their master's side, somber and alert. Not knowing where to direct their attack, they growled at the least noise. Mister Jones was well satisfied by the solicitude of his uneasy guardians.

Finally the sun sank behind the black palms in the arroyo, and in the calm of the silvery night the dogs stationed themselves around the house where Mister Jones was beginning his habitual evening whiskey drinking on the upper floor. At midnight they heard his footsteps, then the double thud of his boots on the wooden floor, and the light went out. There beside the sleeping house the dogs felt alone, closer to the imminent change of owners, and they began to whimper. They whimpered in chorus, pouring out their dry convulsive sobs in a howl of desolation; led by Prince's hunting voice, the others took up the sobbing anew. The puppy barked. Night advanced, and the four older dogs— well fed and caressed by the owner they were about to lose— grouped together in the moonlight, their muzzles pointing heavenward and swollen with laments, to cry out their domestic misery.

The following morning Mister Jones himself went to get the mules and harnessed them to the plow, working until nine o'clock. Even so, he was not satisfied. In addition to the fact that the land had never been well plowed, the blades had no edge, and the plow leapt in the furrow behind the rapid pace of the mules.

He returned to the house with the plow and filed the edges, but a bolt he had noticed was flawed when he bought the plow broke as he was putting it back together. He sent a peon to the neighboring plantation, warning him to be careful of the horse, a good animal, but one extremely sensitive to the sun. Mister Jones raised his head to the melting midday sun and insisted that the peon not gallop one step! He lunched immediately and went upstairs. The dogs, who had not left their master for a second during the morning, lay on the balcony.

The siesta lay heavy upon them, weighted with sunlight and silence; everything was hazy in the burning rays. Around the house the whitish dirt shone like lead in the sun, seeming to lose its contours in the boiling shimmer that closed the blinking eyes of the fox terriers.

"*It* hasn't come back anymore," Milk said.

Old, when he heard *come back*, perked up his ears.

Then, incited by the evocation, the pup stood up and barked, without knowing at what. After a while, he was silent and joined the group in their defensive battle against the flies.

"Nope, *it* didn't come again," Isondú added.

"There was a lizard underneath the tree stump," Prince recalled for the first time.

A hen, beak open, wings held away from its body, crossed the patio at a heavy, heat-slowed lope. Prince followed her lazily with his eyes and then leapt up.

"Here *it* comes again!" he yelled.

Across the patio to the north the horse was returning alone. The dogs arched their backs, barking with prudent fury at Death, which was approaching them. The animal walked with its head hung low, apparently indecisive about what course it should follow. As it passed in the front of the house, it took a few steps in the direction of the well and gradually disappeared in the pitiless light.

Mister Jones came down; he had not been sleepy. He was preparing to repair the plow when unexpectedly he saw the peon on horseback return. To get back so soon he must have been gallop-

15

ing—in spite of his orders. He reproached the peon with all the logic typical of his nationality, reproaches to which the peon responded evasively. Once free, his mission concluded, the poor horse—across whose ribs lay countless lash marks—trembled, lowered his head, and fell on his side. His whip still in his hand, Mister Jones sent the peon to the field to avoid the lashing he would give him if he continued to listen to his Jesuitical excuses. But the dogs were content. Death, who had been searching for their master, had contented itself with the horse. They felt happy, free of worry, and consequently they were starting toward the field when they heard Mister Jones yelling at the peon, far in the distance now, asking him for the bolt. There wasn't any bolt: the store was closed, the owner was sleeping, and so on and so on. Mister Jones, without a word, took his pith helmet from a nail and set out himself in search of the replacement. He was as resistant to the sun as a peon, and the walk would do marvels for his ill humor.

The dogs accompanied him but stopped in the shade of the first carob tree; it was too hot. From there, their feet firmly planted, alert, with worried brow, they watched him walk away from them. Finally, afraid of being left conquered and oppressed by the heat, they trotted after him.

Mister Jones obtained his bolt and returned. To take the shortest route, he avoided the dusty curve of the road and walked in a straight path toward his field. He reached the stream bed and plunged into the hayfield, the diluvial hayfield of the Saladito, which had grown, dried out, and grown up again for as long as there has been hay in the world, without ever knowing fire. The chest-high, arched plants were matted and tangled. The task of crossing through them, difficult enough on a cool day, was extremely difficult at that hour. Pushing his way through the resistant grass, dusty from mud left by floods, Mister Jones was choked by fatigue and billows of bitter nitrate dust.

He emerged, finally, and paused at the edge of the field, but it was impossible, exhausted as he was, to stand still beneath that heat. He continued walking. To the burning heat that had in-

creased without ceasing for three days was now added the suffo-
cation of disordered time. The sky was burning white; not a
breath of air stirred. Mister Jones gasped for air, the pain in his
heart so strong it hurt to breathe.

Mister Jones realized he had exceeded his limits. For some
time he had heard the pounding of his heart in his ears. He felt
dizzy, as if some pressure inside his head were pushing his skull
outward. When he looked at the grass, he grew dizzy. He hurried
forward to reach his house and get out of the sun . . . and then
suddenly came to and found himself in a completely different
place; completely unaware, he had walked a quarter-mile. He
looked around and again felt a new wave of vertigo.

Meanwhile the dogs were following behind him, their tongues
hanging from the sides of their mouths. At times, suffocated,
they would stop in the shade of some esparto grass to sit down,
panting faster than ever, but would then return to the torment
of the sun. Now, almost within reach of the house, they trotted
as fast as they could.

It was at that moment that Old, who was the farthest ahead,
saw Mister Jones through the wire fence, dressed in white, walking toward them. The pup, with a sudden recollection, faced his
patrón and howled, "Death! Death!"

The others had seen it, too, and burst into barking, their hair
standing on end. They saw the figure cross over the wire fence
and for an instant thought they had been mistaken, but when it
came within a hundred meters of them, it stopped, looked at the
group with celestial eyes, and walked straight ahead.

"I hope the *patrón* is on guard!" Prince exclaimed.

"He's going to run right into it!" they all howled.

And, in fact, the figure, after a brief hesitation, advanced, not
directly toward them as before, but in an oblique and apparently
erroneous line that would lead it precisely to an encounter with
Mister Jones. Then the dogs understood that it was all over; their
patrón continued to walk straight ahead like an automaton,
oblivious to everything. Now the figure was upon him. The dogs
lowered their tails and scurried sideways, still howling. A second

passed and the encounter was effected. Mister Jones stopped dead, spun in a circle, and fell to the ground.

The peons, who had seen him fall, hurriedly carried him to the house, but all the water in the world was useless; he died without regaining consciousness. Mister Moore, a stepbrother, came from Buenos Aires, spent an hour in the field, and in four days had liquidated everything and returned immediately to the south. The Indians divided the dogs, who from that time on were thin and mangy and every night, with hungry stealth, went to steal ears of corn in fields not their own.

The Pursued

One night when I was at Lugones's home, the rain so increased in intensity that we rose to look at it from the windows. The wild pampa wind whistled through the wires and whipped the rain in convulsive gusts that distorted the reddish light from the street lamps. This afternoon, after six days of rain, the heavens had cleared to the south, leaving a limpid cold blue sky. And then, behold, the rain returned to promise us another week of bad weather.

Lugones had a stove, which was extremely comforting to my winter debility. We sat down once again and continued our pleasant chat concerning the insane. Several days before, Lugones had visited an insane asylum, and the bizarre behavior of the inmates, added to behavior I myself had once observed, afforded more than enough material for a comfortable vis-à-vis between two sane men.

Given the circumstance of the weather, then, we were rather surprised when the bell at the street door rang. Moments later Lucas Díaz Vélez entered.

This individual has had quite an ominous influence over a period of my life, and that was the night I met him. As is customary, Lugones introduced us by our last names only, so that for some time I didn't know his given name.

Díaz was much slimmer then than he is now. His black clothes —the color of dark maté tea—his sharp face, and his large black eyes gave him a none too common appearance. The eyes, of surprising steadiness and extreme brilliance, especially demanded one's attention. In those days he parted his straight hair in the middle, and, perfectly smoothed down, it looked like a shining helmet.

Vélez spoke very little at first. He crossed his legs, responding only when strictly necessary. At a moment when I had turned toward Lugones, I happened to see that Vélez was observing me. Doubtless in another I would have found this examination following an introduction very natural, but his unwavering attention shocked me.

Soon our conversation came to a standstill. Our situation was not very pleasant, especially for Vélez, since he must have assumed that we were not practicing this terrible muteness before he arrived. He himself broke the silence. He spoke to Lugones of some honey cakes a friend had sent him from Salta, a sample of which he should have brought that night. They seemed to be of a particularly pleasing variety, and, as Lugones showed sufficient interest in sampling them, Díaz Vélez promised to send him the means to do so.

Once the ice was broken, after about ten minutes we returned to our subject of madmen. Although seeming not to lose a single word of what he heard, Díaz held himself apart from the lively subject; perhaps it was not his predilection. As a result, when Lugones left the room for a moment, I was astonished by his unexpected interest. In one minute he told me a number of anecdotes—his expression animated and his mouth precise with conviction. He certainly had much more love for these things than I had supposed, and his last story, related with great vivacity, made me see that he understood the mad with a subtlety not common in this world.

The story was about a boy from the provinces who, after emerging from the debilitating weakness of typhoid, found the streets peopled with enemies. He underwent two months of persecution, committing, as a result, all kinds of foolish acts. As he was a boy of certain intelligence, he commented on his own case so cleverly that it was impossible to know what to think. It sounded exactly like a farce, and this was the general impression of those who heard him discuss his own case so roguishly—always with the vanity characteristic of the mad.

In this fashion he spent three months displaying his psychological astuteness, until one day his mind was cleansed in the clear water of sanity and his ideas became more temperate.

"He is well now," Vélez concluded, "but several rather symptomatic acts have remained with him. A week ago, for example, I ran into him in a pharmacy; he was leaning against the counter, waiting for what I don't know. We started chatting. Suddenly an individual came in without our seeing him, and, as there was no clerk, he rapped with his fingers on the counter. My friend abruptly turned on the intruder with truly animal quickness, staring into his eyes. Anyone would have similarly turned, but not with that rapidity of a man who is always on his guard. Although he was no longer pursued, he must have retained, unawares, an underlying fear that exploded at the least surprise. After staring for a moment, not moving a muscle, he blinked and averted his disinterested eyes. It was as though he had guarded a dark memory of something terrible that happened to him in another time, something he never wanted to catch him unprepared again. Imagine, then, the effect on him of someone's grabbing his arm on the street. I think it would never leave him."

"Undoubtedly the symptom is typical," I confirmed. "And did the psychological talk come to an end also?"

A strange thing: Díaz became very serious and gave me a cold, hostile look.

"May I know why you ask me that?"

"Because we were speaking precisely *of* that!" I replied, surprised. But obviously the man had seen how ridiculous he had been, because immediately he apologized profusely.

"Forgive me. I don't know what happened to me. I've felt this way at times . . . unexpectedly lost my head. Crazy things," he added, laughing and playing with a ruler.

"Completely crazy," I joked.

"And *so* crazy! It's only by chance I have an ounce of sense left. And now I remember, although I asked your pardon—and I ask it again—that I haven't answered your question. My friend does not talk about psychology any more. And now that he is eminently sane, he does not feel perverse in denouncing his own madness as he did before, forcing that terrible two-edged sword one calls reason, you see? It's very clear."

"Not very," I allowed myself to doubt.

"Possibly," he laughed, conclusively. "Another really crazy thing." He winked at me and moved away from the table, smiling and shaking his head like someone who is withholding many things he could tell.

Lugones returned, and we dropped the subject—already exhausted. During the remainder of the visit Díaz spoke very little, although it was clear that his own lack of sociability was making him very nervous. Finally, he left. Perhaps he tried to overcome any bad impression he may have made by his extremely friendly farewell, offering his name and the hospitality of his house along with the prolonged clasp of affectionate hands. Lugones went down with him, since the now-dark stairway was so precipitous that no one was ever tempted to try it alone.

"What the devil kind of person is he?" I asked when Lugones returned. He shrugged his shoulders.

"A terrible individual. I don't know how he came to speak ten words to you tonight. He often sits a whole hour without speaking a word, and you can imagine how pleased I am when he's like that. On the other hand, he comes very seldom. And he's very intelligent in his good moments. You must have noticed that, since I heard you talking."

"Yes, he was telling me about a strange case."

"What case?"

"About a friend who is pursued. He knows as much about madness as the devil himself."

"I guess so, since he himself is pursued."

Scarcely had I heard what he said than a flash of explanatory logic illuminated the darkness I had felt in the other. Undoubtedly . . . ! I remembered above all his irritable air when I asked him if he didn't discuss psychology any more. . . . The good madman had thought I had guessed his secret and was insinuating myself into his consciousness. . . .

"Of course!" I laughed. "Now I understand! But your Díaz

Vélez is fiendishly subtle!" And I told him about the snare he had thrown out to me to amuse himself at my expense: the fiction of a pursued friend, and his comments. But I had scarcely begun when Lugones interrupted.

"There is no friend; that actually happened. Except that his friend is he himself. He told you the complete truth; he had typhoid, was very ill, and is cured to this degree, and now you see that his very sanity is questionable. It's also very possible that the business of the store counter is true, but that it happened to him. He's an interesting individual, eh?"

"And then some!" I responded, as I toyed with the ashtray.

It was late when I left. The weather had finally settled, and, although one could not see the sky above, he sensed the ceiling had lifted. It was no longer raining. A strong, dry wind rippled the water on the sidewalks and forced one to lean into it at street corners. I reached Santa Fe Street and waited a while for the streetcar, shaking the water from my feet. Bored, I decided to walk; I quickened my pace, dug my hands into my pockets, and then thought in some detail about Díaz Vélez.

The thing I remembered best about him was the look with which he had first observed me. It couldn't be called intelligent, reserving intelligence to be included among those qualities—habitual in persons of certain stature—to be *exchanged* to a greater or lesser degree among persons of similar culture. In such looks there is always an interchange of souls: one delves into the depths of the person he has just met and, at the same time, yields part of his own soul to the stranger.

Díaz didn't look at me that way; he only looked *at* me. He wasn't thinking what I was or what I might be, nor was there in his look the least spark of psychological curiosity. He was simply observing me, as one would unblinkingly observe the equivocal attitude of some feline.

After what Lugones had told me, I was no longer astonished by the objectivity of the madman's stare. After his examination, satisfied surely, he had made fun of me, shaking the scarecrow of his own madness in my face. But his desire to denounce himself, without revealing himself, had less the object of making fun of me than of entertaining himself. I was simply a pretext for his argument and, above all, a point of confrontation; the more I admired the devilish perversity of the madman he was describing to me, the more he must have been furtively rubbing his hands. The only thing that kept him from being completely happy was that I didn't say, "But isn't your friend afraid they'll find him out when he denounces himself that way?" It hadn't occurred to me, because the friend didn't interest me especially. But now that I knew who the pursued one was, I promised myself to provide him with the wild happiness he desired. This is what I was thinking as I walked along.

Nevertheless, two weeks passed without my seeing him. I knew through Lugones that he had been at Lugones's house to bring him the confections—a good gift for him.

"He also brought some for you. Since he didn't know where you live—I don't think you gave him your address—he left them at my house. You must come by and get them."

"Some day. Is he still at the same address?"

"Díaz Vélez?"

"Yes."

"Yes, I suppose so; he didn't say a word about leaving."

The next rainy night I went to Lugones's house, sure of finding Díaz Vélez. Even though I realized, better than anyone, that the logic of thinking I would meet him *precisely* on a rainy night was worthy only of a dog or a madman, the probability of absurd coincidence always rules in such cases where reason no longer operates.

Lugones laughed at my insistence on seeing Díaz Vélez.

"Be careful! The pursued always begin by adoring their future victims. He remembered you very well."

"That doesn't matter. When I see him, it's going to be *my* turn to amuse myself."

I left very late that night.

But I didn't find Díaz Vélez. Not until one noon when, just as I was starting to cross the street, I saw him on Artes Street. He was walking north, looking into all the shopwindows, not missing a one, like a person preoccupied. When I caught a glimpse of him, I had one foot off the sidewalk. I tried to stop, but I couldn't, and I stepped into the street, almost stumbling. I turned around and looked at the curb, although I was quite sure there was nothing there. One of the plaza carriages driven by a Negro in a shiny jacket passed so close to me that the hub of the rear wheel left grease on my trousers. I stood still, staring at the horse's hooves, until an automobile forced me to jump out of the way.

All this lasted about ten seconds, as Díaz continued moving away, and I was forced to hurry. When I felt sure of overtaking him, all my hesitation left and was replaced by a great feeling of self-satisfaction. I felt myself in perfect equilibrium. All my nerves were tingling and resilient. I opened and closed my hands, flexing my fingers, happy. Four or five times a minute I put my hand to my watch, forgetting that it was broken.

Díaz Vélez continued walking, and soon I was two steps behind him. One step more and I *could* touch him. But seeing him this way, not even remotely aware of my presence in spite of his delirium about persecution and psychology, I adjusted my step exactly to his. Pursued! Very well . . . ! I noted in detail his head, his elbows, his clenched hands—held a little away from his body —the transverse wrinkles of his trousers at the back of the knee, the heels of his shoes, appearing and disappearing. I had the dizzying sensation that once before, millions of years before, I had done this: met Díaz Vélez in the street, followed him, caught up with him, and, having done so, continued to follow behind him— *behind him*. I glowed with the satisfaction of a dozen lifetimes. Why touch him? Suddenly it occurred to me that he might turn around, and instantly anguish clutched at my throat. I thought that with my larynx throttled like this I wouldn't be able to cry out, and my only fear, my terrifyingly unique fear, was that I would not be able to cry out if he turned around, as if the goal of my existence were suddenly to throw myself upon him, to pry open his jaws, and to shout unrestrainedly into his open mouth—counting every molar as I yelled.

I had such a moment of anguish that I forgot that it was *he* I was seeing: Díaz Vélez's arms, Díaz Vélez's legs, Díaz Vélez's hair, Díaz Vélez's hatband, the woof of Díaz Vélez's hatband, the warp of the warp of Díaz Vélez, Díaz Vélez, Díaz Vélez. . . .

The realization that, in spite of my terror, I hadn't missed one moment of him, Díaz Vélez, assured me completely.

A moment later I was possessed by the mad temptation to touch him without his noticing it, and immediately, filled with the greatest happiness one's own original creative act can hold, softly, exquisitely, I touched his jacket, just on the lower edge—no more, no less. I touched it and plunged my closed fist into my pocket.

I am sure that more than ten people saw me. I was aware of three. One of them, walking in the opposite direction along the sidewalk across the street, kept turning around with amused surprise. In his hand he was carrying a valise that pointed toward me every time he turned.

Another was a streetcar inspector who was standing on the curb, his legs spread wide apart. From his expression I understood that he had been watching us even before I did it. He did not manifest the least surprise or change his stance or move his head, but he certainly did follow us with his eyes. I assumed he was an elderly employee who had learned to see only what suited him.

The third person was a heavy individual with magnificent bearing, a Catalan-style beard, and eyeglasses with gold frames. He must have been a businessman in Spain. He was just passing us, and he saw me do it. I was sure he had stopped. Sure enough, when we reached the corner, I turned around and I saw him, standing still, staring at me with a rich honorable bourgeois look, frowning, with his head thrown back slightly. This individual enchanted me. Two steps later, I turned my head and laughed in his face. I saw that he frowned even more and drew himself up with dignity as if he doubted whether he could be the one intended. I made a vague, nonsensical gesture that disorganized him completely.

I followed Díaz Vélez, once again attentive only to him. Now we had crossed Cuyo, Corrientes, Lavalle, Tucumán, and Viamonte (the affair of the jacket and the three looks had occurred between the latter two). Three minutes later we had reached Charcas, and there Díaz stopped. He looked toward Suipacha, detected a silhouette behind him, and suddenly turned around. I remember this detail perfectly: for a half-second he gazed at one of the buttons on my jacket, a rapid glance, preoccupied and vague at the same time, like someone who suddenly focuses on one object, just at the point of remembering something else. Almost immediately he looked into my eyes.

"Oh, how are you!" he clasped my hand, shaking it rapidly. "I haven't had the pleasure of seeing you since that night at Lugones's. Were you coming down Artes?"

"Yes. I turned in at Viamonte and was hurrying to catch up with you. I've been hoping to see you."

"And I, you. Haven't you been back by Lugones's?"

"Yes, and thank you for the honey cakes; delicious."

We stood silent, looking at each other.

"How are you getting along?" I burst out, smiling, expressing in the question more affection than real desire to know how he was.

"Very well," he replied in a similar tone. And we smiled at each other again.

As soon as we had begun to talk, I had lost the disturbing flashes of gaiety of a few moments before. I was calm again and, certainly, filled with tenderness for Díaz Vélez. I think I had never looked at anyone with more affection than I did at him on that occasion.

"Were you waiting for the streetcar?"

"Yes," he nodded, looking at the time. As he lowered his head to look at his watch, I saw fleetingly that the tip of his nose touched the edge of his upper lip. Warm affection for Díaz swelled from my heart.

"Wouldn't you like to have some coffee? There's a marvelous sun. . . . That is, if you've already eaten and are in no hurry . . ."

"Yes, no, no hurry," he answered distractedly, looking down the tracks into the distance.

We turned back. He didn't seem entirely delighted at the prospect of accompanying me. I wished he were happier and more subtle—especially more subtle. Nevertheless, my effusive tenderness for him so animated my voice that after three blocks Díaz began to change. Until then he had done nothing but pull at his right mustache with his left hand, nodding, but not looking at me. From then on he began to gesticulate with both hands. By the time we reached Corrientes Street—I don't know what damned thing I had said to him—he smiled almost imperceptibly, focusing alternately on the moving toes of my shoes, and gave me a fleeting glance from the corner of his eye.

"Hum . . . now it begins," I thought. And my ideas, in perfect order until that moment, began to shift and crash into each other dizzily. I made an effort to pull myself together, and I suddenly remembered a lead cat sitting on a chair that I had seen when I was five years old. Why that cat? I whistled and quickly stopped. Then I blew my nose and laughed secretly behind my handkerchief. As I had lowered my head, and the handkerchief was large, only my eyes could be seen. And then I peeked at Díaz Vélez, so sure he wouldn't see me that I had the overwhelming temptation to spit hastily into my hand three times and laugh out loud, just to do something crazy.

By now we were in La Brasileña. We sat down across from one another at a tiny little table, our knees almost touching. In the half-dark, the Nile green color of the café gave such a strong impression of damp and sparkling freshness that one felt obliged to examine the walls to see if they were wet.

Díaz shifted in his chair toward the waiter, who was leaning against the counter with his towel over his crossed arms, and settled into a comfortable position.

We sat for a while without speaking, but the flies of excitement were constantly buzzing through my brain. Although I felt serious, a convulsive smile kept rising to my lips. When we had sat down, I had bitten my lips trying to adopt a normal expression, but this overwhelming tic kept breaking through. My ideas rushed headlong in an unending procession, piling onto one another with undreamed-of velocity; each idea represented an uncontrollable impulse to create ridiculous and, especially, unexpected situations; I had a mad desire to undertake each one, then stop suddenly, and begin another: to poke my forked fingers in Díaz Vélez's eyes, to pull my hair and yell just for the hell of it, and all just to do something absurd—especially to Díaz Vélez. Two or three times I glanced at him and then dropped my eyes. My face must have been crimson because I could feel it burning.

All this occurred during the time it took the waiter to come with his little machine, serve the coffee, and go away, first glancing absent-mindedly into the street. Díaz was still out of sorts, which made me think that when I had stopped him on Charcas Street he had been thinking about something quite different from accompanying a madman like me. . . .

That was it! I had just stumbled onto the reason for my uneasiness: Díaz Vélez, a damned and pursued madman, knew perfectly well that he was responsible for my recent behavior. "I'm sure that my friend," he must have said to himself, "will have the puerile notion of wanting to frighten me when next we see each other. If he happens to find me, he'll pretend to have sudden impulses, psychological manifestations, a persecution complex; he'll follow me down the street making faces; he will then take me somewhere to buy me a cup of coffee. . . ."

"You are com-plete-ly wrong," I told him, putting my elbows on the table and resting my chin in my hands. I looked at him— smiling, no doubt—but never taking my eyes off him.

Díaz seemed to be surprised that I had come out with this unexpected remark.

"What do you mean?"

"Nothing. Just this: you are com-plete-ly wrong!"

"But what the devil do you mean? It's possible that I'm wrong, I guess. . . . Undoubtedly, it's very probable that I'm wrong!"

"It's not a question of whether you guess, or whether there's any doubt. What I'm saying is this—and I'm going to repeat it carefully so you'll be sure to understand—you-are-com-plete-ly-wrong!"

This time Díaz, jovially attentive, looked at me and then burst out laughing and glanced away.

"All right, let's agree on it!"

"You do well to agree, because that's the way it is," I persisted, my chin still in my hands.

"I think so, too," he laughed again.

But I was very sure the damned fellow knew exactly what I meant. The more I stared at him, the more dizzily the ideas were careening about in my head.

"Dí-az Vé-lez," I articulated slowly, not for an instant removing my eyes from his. Díaz, understanding that I wasn't addressing him, continued to look straight ahead.

"Dí-az Vé-lez," I repeated with the same incurious vagueness, as if a third, invisible person sitting with us had intervened.

Díaz, pensive, seemed not to have heard. And suddenly he turned with a look of frankness; his hands were trembling slightly.

"Look," he said with a decided smile. "It would be good if we terminated this interview for today. You're acting badly and I'll end up doing the same. But first it would be helpful if we spoke to each other frankly, because if we don't we will *never* understand each other. To be brief: you and Lugones and everyone think I'm pursued; is that right or not?"

He continued to stare at me, still with the smile of a sincere friend who wants to eliminate forever any misunderstandings. I had expected many things, anything but this boldness. With these words, Díaz placed all his cards on the table, and we sat face to face, observing each other's every gesture. He knew that *I knew* he wanted to play with me again, as he had the first night at Lugones's, but nevertheless he dared incite me.

Suddenly I became calm; it was no longer a matter of letting the flies of excitement race surreptitiously through my own brain

32

and waiting to see what would happen, but of stilling the swarm in my own mind in order to listen attentively to the buzzing in another's.

"Perhaps," I responded vaguely when he had completed his question.

"*You* thought I was pursued, didn't you?"

"I thought so."

"And that a certain story I told you at Lugones's about a mad friend of mine was to amuse myself at your expense?"

"Yes."

"Forgive me for continuing. Lugones told you something about me?"

"He did."

"That I was pursued?"

"Yes."

"And you believe, more than you did before, that I am, don't you?"

"Exactly."

Both of us burst out laughing, each looking away at the same instant. Díaz lifted his cup to his lips, but in the middle of the gesture noticed that it was empty and set it down. His eyes were even more brilliant than usual, with dark circles beneath them— not like those of a man, but large and purplish like a woman's.

"All right, all right," he shook his head cordially. "It's difficult *not* to believe it. It's possible, just as possible as what I'm going to tell you. Listen carefully: I may or I may not be pursued, but what is certain is that your eagerness that I see that *you* are too will have this result: in your desire to study me, you will make me truly pursued, and then I will occupy myself in making faces at *you* when you're not looking, as you did to me for six blocks only a half-hour ago . . . which certainly is true. And there is another possible consequence: we understand each other very well; you know that I—an *intelligent* and truly pursued person—am capable of feigning a miraculous normality; and I know that you—in the larval stage of persecution—are capable of simulating perfect fear. Do you agree?"

"Yes, it's possible there's something in that."

"Something? No, everything!"

We laughed again, each immediately looking away. I put my elbows on the table and my chin in my hands, as I had a while before.

"And if I truly believe that you are following me?"

I saw those two brilliant eyes fixed on mine.

In the exchange of our glances there was nothing but the perverse question that had betrayed him, the brief suspension of his shrewdness. Did he mean to ask me that? No, but his madness was so far advanced that he could not resist the temptation. He smiled as he asked his subtle question, but the madman, the real madman, had escaped and was peering at me from behind his eyes.

I shrugged my shoulders carelessly, and, like someone who casually places his hand on the table when he is going to shift his position, I surreptitiously picked up the sugar bowl. But the moment I did it, I felt ashamed and put it down. Díaz watched it all without flickering an eyelid.

"Just the same, you were afraid," he smiled.

"No," I replied happily, drawing my chair a little closer. "It was an act, one that any good friend might put on—any friend with whom one has an *understanding*."

I knew that *he* wasn't putting on an act and that behind the intelligent eyes directing the subtle game still crouched the mad assassin, like a dark beast seeking shelter that sends out decoy cubs on reconnaissance. Little by little the beast was withdrawing, and sanity began to shine in his eyes. Once again he became master of himself; he ran his hand over his shining hair, and, laughing for the last time, he stood up.

It was already two o'clock. We walked toward Charcas talking about various things, in mutual tacit agreement to limit the conversation to ordinary things—the sort of brief, casual dialogue a married couple maintains on the streetcar.

As is always true in these circumstances, once we stopped neither of us spoke for a moment, and, also as always, the first thing we said had nothing to do with our farewell.

"This asphalt is in bad shape," I ventured, pointing with my chin.

"Yes, it never is any good," he replied in a similar tone. "When shall we see each other again?"

"Soon. Won't you be going by Lugones's?"

"Who knows. . . . Tell me, where the devil do you live? I don't remember."

I gave him the address. "Do you plan to come by?"

"Some day . . ."

As we shook hands, we couldn't help exchanging a look, and we burst out laughing together for the hundredth time in two hours.

"Good-by, be seeing you."

After a few feet, I walked very deliberately for a few paces and looked over my shoulder. Díaz had turned around, too. We exchanged a last salute, he with his left hand and I with my right, and then we both walked a little faster.

The madman, the damned madman! I could still see his look in the café. I'd seen it clearly. I'd seen the brutish and suspicious madman behind the actor who was arguing with me! So he'd seen me following him in the glass of the shopwindows! Once again I felt a deep need to provoke him, to make him see clearly that *he* was beginning now, he was losing confidence in me, that any day he was going to want to do to me what I was doing to him. . . .

I was alone in my room. It was late and the house was sleeping; in the entire house there was not a sound to be heard. My sensation of isolation was so strong that unconsciously I raised my eyes and looked around. The incandescent gaslight coldly and peacefully illuminated the walls. I looked at the cone and ascertained that it was not burning with the usual small popping. Everything was deathly still.

It is well known that one has only to repeat a word aloud six or seven times for it to lose all meaning and for it to be converted into a new and absolutely incomprehensible utterance. That is what happened to me. I was alone, alone, alone. . . . What does *alone* mean? And as I looked up I saw a man standing in the doorway looking at me.

I stopped breathing for an instant. I was familiar with the sensation, and I knew that immediately the hair would rise at the back of my neck. I lowered my eyes, continuing my letter, but out of the corner of my eye I saw that the man had appeared again. I knew very well that it was nothing. But I couldn't help myself and, suddenly, I looked. That I looked meant I was lost.

And all of this was Díaz's work; he had got me overexcited about his stupid persecutions, and now I was paying for it.

I pretended not to notice and continued writing, but the man was still there. From that instant, in the lighted silence and the empty space behind me surged the annihilating anguish of a man who is alone in an empty house but doesn't feel alone. And it wasn't only this; *things* were standing behind me. I continued my letter, but the eyes were still in the doorway and the things were almost touching me. Gradually the profound terror I was trying to contain made my hair stand on end, and, rising to my feet as naturally as one is capable in such circumstances, I went to the door and opened it wide. But I know what it cost me to do it slowly.

I didn't pretend to return to my writing. Díaz Vélez! There was no other reason why my nerves should be like this. But I was completely certain, too, that—an eye for an eye and a tooth for a tooth—he was going to pay for all this evening's pleasures.

The door to the street was still open, and I listened to the bustle of people leaving the theaters. "He could have attended one of them," I thought. "And since he has to take the Charcas streetcar, it's possible he passed by here. . . . And if it's his idea to annoy me with his ridiculous games, pretending he already feels himself pursued and knowing that I'm beginning to believe he is . . ."

Someone knocked at the door.

He! I leaped back into my room and extinguished the lamp in a flash. I stood very still, holding my breath. My skin tingled painfully as I awaited a second knock.

He knocked again. And then after a while I heard his steps advancing across the patio. They stopped at my door, and the intruder stood motionless before its darkness. Of course there was no one there. Then suddenly he called me. Damn him! He knew that I had heard him, that I had turned out the light when I heard, and that I was standing, not moving, by the table! He knew *precisely* what I was thinking, and that I was waiting, waiting, as in a nightmare, to hear my name called once again!

He called me a second time. Then, after a long pause, "Horacio!"

Damnation! What did my name have to do with all this? What right did he have to call me Horacio, he who in spite of his tormenting wickedness would not come in because he was afraid! "He knows that this is what I am thinking at this instant; he is convinced of it, but the madness is upon him, and he won't come in!"

And he didn't. He stood an instant more before he moved away from the threshold and returned to the entrance hall. Rapidly, I left the table, tiptoed to the door, and stuck out my head. "He knows I'm going to do this." Nevertheless, he continued at a tranquil pace and disappeared.

Considering what had just happened, I appreciated the superhuman effort the pursued one made in not turning around, knowing that behind his back I was devouring him with my eyes.

One week later I received this letter:

My dear X:
Because of a bad cold, I haven't been out for four days. If you are not afraid of the contagion, you would give me great pleasure by coming to chat with me for a while.
> Yours very truly,
> Lucas Díaz Vélez

P.S. If you see Lugones, tell him I have been sent something that will interest him very much.

37

I received the letter at two o'clock in the afternoon. As it was cold and I was planning to go for a walk, I hurried over to Lugones's.

"What are you doing here at this time of day?" he asked me. I didn't see him very frequently in the afternoon in those days.

"Nothing. Díaz Vélez sends you his regards."

"So it's still you and Díaz Vélez," he laughed.

"Yes, still. I just received a letter from him. It seems he hasn't been out of the house for four days."

It was evident to both of us that this was the beginning of the end, and in five minutes' speculation on the matter we had invented a million absurd things that could have happened to Díaz. But since I hadn't told Lugones about my hectic day with Díaz, his interest was soon exhausted and I left.

For the same reason, Lugones understood very little about my visit. It was unthinkable that I had gone to his house expressly to tell him that Díaz was offering him more honey cakes; and, since I had left almost immediately, the man must have been thinking everything except what was really at the heart of the matter.

At eight o'clock I knocked at Vélez's door. I gave my name to the servant, and a few moments later an elderly lady, obviously from the provinces, appeared. Her hair was smooth, and she was wearing a black dressing gown with an interminable row of covered buttons.

"Do you want to see Lucas?" she asked, looking at me suspiciously.

"Yes, ma'am."

"He is somewhat ill; I don't know whether he will be able to receive you."

I objected that nonetheless I had received a note from him. The old lady looked at me again.

"Please be good enough to wait a moment."

She returned and led me to my friend. Díaz was sitting up in bed with a jacket over his nightshirt. He introduced us to each other.

"My aunt . . ."

When she withdrew, I said, "I thought you lived alone."

"I used to, but she's been living here with me for the last two months. Bring up a chair."

The moment I saw him I was sure that what Lugones and I had conjectured was true; he absolutely did not have a cold.

"Bronchitis . . . ?"

"Yes, something like that. . . ."

I took a quick look around. The room was like any other room with whitewashed walls. He, too, had incandescent gas. I looked with curiosity at the cone, but his whistled, whereas mine popped. As for the rest, a beautiful silence throughout the house.

When I looked back at him, he was watching me. It must have been at least five seconds that he had been watching me. Our glances locked, and a shiver sent its tentacles to the marrow of my bones. But he was completely mad now! The pursued one was living just behind Díaz's eyes. The only thing, absolutely the only thing in his eyes was a murderous fixation.

"He's going to attack me," I agonized to myself. But the obstinacy suddenly disappeared, and after a quick glance at the ceiling Díaz recovered his habitual expression. He looked at me, smiling, and then dropped his eyes.

"Why didn't you answer me the other evening in your room?"

"I don't know."

"Do you think I didn't come in because I was afraid?"

"Something like that."

"But do you think I'm not really ill?"

"No. . . . Why?"

He raised his arm and let it fall lazily on the quilt.

"I was looking at you a little bit ago. . . ."

"Let's forget it, shall we!"

"The madman had escaped from me, hadn't he?"

"Forget it, Díaz, forget it!"

I had a knot in my throat. His every word had the effect on me of one more push toward an imminent abyss.

If he continues, he'll explode! He won't be able to hold it back!

And then I clearly realized that Lugones and I had been right. Díaz had taken to his bed because he was afraid! I looked at him and shuddered violently. There it was again! The assassin was once more staring through eyes now fixed on me. But, as before, after a glance at the ceiling, the light of normalcy returned to them.

"One thing is certain, it's fiendishly quiet here," I said to myself.

A moment passed.

"Do you like the silence?"

"Absolutely."

"It's funereal. Suddenly you get the sensation that there are things concentrating too much on you. Let me give you an example."

"What do you mean?"

His eyes were shining with perverse intelligence as they had at other times.

"Well, suppose that you, like me, have been alone, in bed, for four days, and that you—I mean, I—haven't thought about you. Suppose you hear a voice clearly, not yours, not mine, a clear voice, anywhere, behind the wardrobe, in the ceiling—here in this ceiling, for example—calling you, insult——"

He stopped: he was staring at the ceiling, his face completely altered by hatred, and then he shouted, "There are! There are!"

Shaken to my soul, I instantly recalled his former glances; he heard the voice that insulted him from the ceiling, but I was the one who pursued him. No doubt he still possessed discernment enough not to link the two things together.

His face had been suffused with color. Now, by contrast, Díaz had become frightfully pale. Finally, with an effort, he turned away from the ceiling and lay quietly for a moment, his expression vague and his breathing agitated.

I could not remain there any longer. I glanced at the night table and saw the half-open drawer.

"As soon as I stand up," I thought with anguish, "he's going to shoot me dead." But in spite of everything, I rose and ap-

40

proached him to say good-by. Díaz, with a sudden start, turned toward me. In the time it took me to reach his side, his breathing stopped and his fascinated eyes took on the expression of a cornered animal watching the sights of a shotgun drawing near.

"I hope you feel better, Díaz. . . ."

I did not dare hold out my hand, but reason is as violent as madness and is extremely painful to lose. Díaz came to his senses and extended *his* hand.

"Come tomorrow; I'm not well today."

"I'm afraid I . . ."

"No, no, come. Come!" he concluded with imperious anguish.

I left without seeing anyone, feeling, as I found myself free and remembering with horror that extremely intelligent man battling with the ceiling, that I was cured forever of psychological games.

The following day, at eight o'clock in the evening, a boy delivered this note to me:

> Sir:
> Lucas insists on seeing you. If it wouldn't be a bother I would appreciate your stopping by here today.
> Hoping to hear from you,
> Desolinda S. de Roldán

I had had a disturbing day. I couldn't think about Díaz that I didn't see him shouting again during that horrible loss of conscious reason. His nerves were strung so tight that a sudden blast from a train whistle would have shattered them.

I went, nevertheless, but as I walked along I found I was painfully shaken by the least noise. So when I turned the corner and saw a group in front of Díaz Vélez's door, my legs grew weak—not from any concrete fear, but from coincidences, from things foreseen, from cataclysms of logic.

I heard a murmur of fear.

"He's coming; he's coming!" And everyone scattered into the middle of the street.

"There it is; he's mad," I said to myself, grieved by what might have happened. I ran, and in a moment I stood before the door.

Díaz lived on Arenales Street between Bulnes and Vidt. The house had an extensive interior patio overflowing with plants. As there was no light in the patio, as contrasted with the entryway, the patio beyond lay in deep shadow.

"What's going on?" I asked.

Several persons replied:

"The young man who lives here is crazy."

"He's wandering around the patio. . . ."

"He's naked. . . ."

"He keeps running out. . . ."

I was anxious to know about his aunt.

"There she is."

I turned, and there against the window was the poor lady, sobbing. When she saw me she redoubled her weeping.

"Lucas . . . ! He's gone mad!"

"When?"

"Just a while ago. . . . He came running out of his room . . . shortly after I had sent you . . ."

I felt someone was speaking to me.

"Listen, listen!"

From the black depths of the patio we heard a pitiful cry.

"He yells like that every few minutes. . . ."

"Here he comes; here he comes!" everyone shouted, fleeing.

I didn't have time or strength to run away. I felt a muffled, precipitous rush, and Díaz Vélez, livid, completely nude, his eyes bulging out of his head, rushed into the entrance hall, carried me along in front of him, made a ridiculous grimace in the doorway, and ran back into the patio.

"Get out of there; he'll kill you," they yelled at me. "He shot at a chair today."

Everyone had clustered around the door again, peering into the shadows.

"Listen . . . , again."

Now it was a cry of agony that emerged from the depths. "Water . . . ! Water . . . !"

42

"He's asked for water two times."

The two officers who had just arrived had decided to post themselves on either side of the entrance hall at the rear and seize Díaz the next time he rushed into the hall. The wait was even more agonizing this time. But soon the cry was repeated, and, following it, the scattering of the crowd.

"Here he comes!"

Díaz rushed out, violently hurled an empty vase into the street, and an instant later was subdued. He defended himself fiercely, but, when he saw it was hopeless to resist, he stopped struggling, astonished and panting, and looked from person to person with surprise. He did not recognize me, nor did I delay there any longer.

The following morning I went to have lunch with Lugones and told him the whole story—this time we were very serious.

"What a shame; he was very intelligent."

"Too intelligent," I confirmed, remembering.

All this was June 1903.

"Let's do something," Lugones said to me. "Why don't we go to Misiones? That will give us something to do."

We went, and four months later we returned, Lugones with a full beard and I with a ruined stomach.

Díaz was in an institution. Since the crisis, which had lasted two days, there had been no further incidents. When I went to visit him, he received me effusively.

"I thought I'd never see you again. Have you been away?"

"Yes, for a while. Getting along all right?"

"Just fine. I hope to be completely well before the end of the year."

I couldn't help looking at him.

"Yes," he smiled. "Although I feel fine, I think it's prudent to wait a few months. But deep down, since that night, nothing has happened."

"Do you remember . . . ?"

"No, but they told me about it. I must have been quite a sight, naked."

We entertained ourselves a while longer.

"Look," he said seriously, "I'm going to ask you a favor: come see me often. You don't know how these gentlemen bore me with their innocent questions and their snares. All they succeed in doing is making me bitter, eliciting ideas from me that I don't like to remember. I'm sure that in the company of someone a little more intelligent I will be wholly cured."

I solemnly promised him to do it, and for two months I returned frequently, never denouncing the least fault, sometimes even touching on our old relationship.

One day I found an intern with him. Díaz winked lightly and gravely introduced me to his guardian. The three of us chatted like judicious friends. Nevertheless, I noted in Díaz Vélez—with some pleasure, I admit—a certain fiendish irony in everything he was saying to his doctor. He adroitly directed the conversation to the patients and soon placed his own case before us.

"But you are different," objected the doctor. "You're cured."

"Not really, if you consider that I still have to be here."

"A simple precaution . . . you understand that yourself."

"But what's the reason for it? Don't you think it will be impossible, absolutely impossible, ever to know when I'm sane—with no need for 'precaution,' as you say. I can't be, I believe, more sane than I am now."

"Not as far as I can see," the doctor laughed happily.

Díaz gave me another imperceptible wink.

"It seems to me that one cannot have any greater conscious sanity than this—permit me: You both know, as I do, that I have been pursued, that one night I had a crisis, that I have been here six months, and that *any* amount of time is short for an absolute guarantee that the thing won't return. Fine. This 'precaution' would be sensible if I didn't see all this clearly and discuss it intelligently. . . . I know that at this moment you are recalling cases of lucid madness and are comparing me to that madman in La Plata. The one who in bad moments quite naturally made fun of a broom he thought was his wife but, when completely himself and laughing, still kept his eyes on the broom, so that no one would touch it. . . . I know, too, that this objective perspicacity in following the doctor's opinion while recounting a similar case to one's own is itself madness . . . and the very astuteness of the analysis only confirms it. . . . But . . . even so—in what manner, in what other way, may a sane man defend himself?"

"There is no other way, absolutely none," the intern who was being interrogated burst out laughing. Díaz glanced at me out of the corner of his eye and shrugged his shoulders, smiling.

I had a strong desire to know what the doctor thought about this superlucidity. At a different time I would have valued such lucidity even at the cost of disordering my nerves. I glanced at the doctor, but the man didn't seem to have felt its influence. A moment later we left.

"Do you think . . . ?" I asked him.

"Hum! I think so . . . ," he replied, looking sideways at the patio. Abruptly, he turned his head.

"Look, look!" he told me, pressing my arm.

Díaz, pale, his eyes dilated with terror and hatred, was cautiously approaching the door, as he had surely done every time I came—*looking at me!*

"Ah! You hoodlum!" he yelled at me, raising his fist. "I've been watching you come for two months now!"

The Decapitated Chicken

All day long the four idiot sons of the couple Mazzini-Ferraz sat on a bench in the patio. Their tongues protruded from between their lips; their eyes were dull; their mouths hung open as they turned their heads.

The patio had an earthen floor and was closed to the west by a brick wall. The bench was five feet from the wall, parallel to it, and there they sat, motionless, their gaze fastened on the bricks. As the sun went down, disappearing behind the wall, the idiots rejoiced. The blinding light was always what first gained their attention; little by little their eyes lighted up; finally, they would laugh uproariously, each infected by the same uneasy hilarity, staring at the sun with bestial joy, as if it were something to eat.

Other times, lined up on the bench, they hummed for hours on end, imitating the sound of the trolley. Loud noises, too, shook them from their inertia, and at those times they ran around the patio, biting their tongues and mewing. But almost always they were sunk in the somber lethargy of idiocy, passing the entire day seated on their bench, their legs hanging motionless, dampening their pants with slobber.

The oldest was twelve and the youngest eight. Their dirty and slovenly appearance was testimony to the total lack of maternal care.

These four idiots, nevertheless, had once been the joy of their parents' lives. When they had been married three months, Mazzini and Berta had oriented the self-centered love of man and wife, wife and husband, toward a more vital future: a son. What greater happiness for two people in love than that blessed consecration of an affection liberated from the vile egotism of purposeless love and—what is worse for love itself—love without any possible hope of renewal?

So thought Mazzini and Berta, and, when after fourteen months of matrimony their son arrived, they felt their happiness complete. The child prospered, beautiful and radiant, for a year and a half. But one night in his twentieth month he was racked by terrible convulsions, and the following morning he no longer recognized his parents. The doctor examined him with the kind of professional attention that obviously seeks to find the cause of the illness in the infirmities of the parents.

After a few days the child's paralyzed limbs recovered their movement, but the soul, the intelligence, even instinct, were gone forever. He lay on his mother's lap, an idiot, driveling, limp, to all purposes dead.

"Son, my dearest son!" the mother sobbed over the frightful ruin of her first-born.

The father, desolate, accompanied the doctor outside.

"I can say it to you; I think it is a hopeless case. He might improve, be educated to the degree his idiocy permits, but nothing more."

"Yes! Yes . . . !" Mazzini assented. "But tell me: do you think it is heredity, that . . . ?"

"As far as the paternal heredity is concerned, I told you what I thought when I saw your son. As for the mother's, there's a lung there that doesn't sound too good. I don't see anything else, but her breathing is slightly ragged. Have her thoroughly examined."

With his soul tormented by remorse, Mazzini redoubled his love for his son, the idiot child who was paying for the excesses of his grandfather. At the same time he had to console, to ceaselessly sustain Berta, who was wounded to the depths of her being by the failure of her young motherhood.

As is only natural, the couple put all their love into the hopes for another son. A son was born, and his health and the clarity of his laughter rekindled their extinguished hopes. But at eighteen months the convulsions of the first-born were repeated, and on the following morning the second son awoke an idiot.

This time the parents fell into complete despair. So it was their blood, their love, that was cursed. Especially their love! He, twenty-eight; she, twenty-two; and all their passionate tenderness had not succeeded in creating one atom of normal life. They no longer asked for beauty and intelligence as for the first-born— only a son, a son like any other!

From the second disaster burst forth new flames of aching love, a mad desire to redeem once and for all the sanctity of their tenderness. Twins were born; and step by step the history of the two older brothers was repeated.

Even so, beyond the immense bitterness, Mazzini and Berta maintained great compassion for their four sons. They must wrest from the limbo of deepest animality, not their souls, lost now, but instinct itself. The boys could not swallow, move about, or even sit up. They learned, finally, to walk, but they bumped into things because they took no notice of obstacles. When they were washed, they mewed and gurgled until their faces were flushed. They were animated only by food or when they saw brilliant colors or heard thunder. Then they laughed, radiant with bestial frenzy, pushing out their tongues and spewing rivers of slaver. On the other hand, they possessed a certain imitative faculty, but nothing more.

The terrifying line of descent seemed to have been ended with the twins. But with the passage of three years Mazzini and Berta once again ardently desired another child, trusting that the long interim would have appeased their destiny.

Their hopes were not satisfied. And because of this burning desire and exasperation from its lack of fulfillment, the husband and wife grew bitter. Until this time each had taken his own share of responsibility for the misery their children caused, but hopelessness for the redemption of the four animals born to them finally created that imperious necessity to blame others that is the specific patrimony of inferior hearts.

It began with a change of pronouns: *your* sons. And since they intended to trap, as well as insult each other, the atmosphere became charged.

"It seems to me," Mazzini, who had just come in and was

51

washing his hands, said to Berta, "that you could keep the boys cleaner."

As if she hadn't heard him, Berta continued reading.

"It's the first time," she replied after a pause, "I've seen you concerned about the condition of your sons."

Mazzini turned his head toward her with a forced smile.

"Our sons, I think."

"All right, our sons. Is that the way you like it?" She raised her eyes.

This time Mazzini expressed himself clearly.

"Surely you're not going to say *I'm* to blame, are you?"

"Oh, no!" Berta smiled to herself, very pale. "But neither am I, I imagine! That's all I needed . . . ," she murmured.

"What? What's all you needed?"

"Well, if anyone's to blame, it isn't me, just remember that! That's what I meant."

Her husband looked at her for a moment with a brutal desire to wound her.

"Let's drop it!" he said finally, drying his hands.

"As you wish, but if you mean . . ."

"Berta!"

"As you wish!"

This was the first clash, and others followed. But, in the inevitable reconciliations, their souls were united in redoubled rapture and eagerness for another child.

So a daughter was born. Mazzini and Berta lived for two years with anguish as their constant companion, always expecting another disaster. It did not occur, however, and the parents focused all their contentment on their daughter, who took advantage of their indulgence to become spoiled and very badly behaved.

Although even in the later years Berta had continued to care for the four boys, after Bertita's birth she virtually ignored the other children. The very thought of them horrified her, like the memory of something atrocious she had been forced to perform. The same thing happened to Mazzini, though to a lesser degree.

Nevertheless, their souls had not found peace. Their daughter's least indisposition now unleashed—because of the terror of losing her—the bitterness created by their unsound progeny. Bile had accumulated for so long that the distended viscera spilled venom at the slightest touch. From the moment of the first poisonous quarrel Mazzini and Berta had lost respect for one another, and if there is anything to which man feels himself drawn with cruel fulfillment it is, once begun, the complete humiliation of another person. Formerly they had been restrained by their mutual failure; now that success had come, each, attributing it to himself, felt more strongly the infamy of the four misbegotten sons the other had forced him to create.

With such emotions there was no longer any possibility of affection for the four boys. The servant dressed them, fed them, put them to bed, with gross brutality. She almost never bathed them. They spent most of the day facing the wall, deprived of anything resembling a caress.

So Bertita celebrated her fourth birthday, and that night, as a result of the sweets her parents were incapable of denying her, the child had a slight chill and fever. And the fear of seeing her die or become an idiot opened once again the ever-present wound.

For three hours they did not speak to each other, and, as usual, Mazzini's swift pacing served as a motive.

"My God! Can't you walk more slowly? How many times . . . ?"

"All right, I just forget. I'll stop. I don't do it on purpose."

She smiled, disdainful.

"No, no, of course I don't think that of you!"

"And I would never have believed that of you . . . you consumptive!"

"What! What did you say?"

"Nothing!"

"Oh, yes, I heard you say something! Look, I don't know what you said, but I swear I'd prefer anything to having a father like yours!"

Mazzini turned pale.

"At last!" he muttered between clenched teeth. "At last, viper, you've said what you've been wanting to!"

"Yes, a viper, yes! But I had healthy parents, you hear? Healthy! *My* father didn't die in delirium! I could have had sons like anybody else's! Those are *your* sons, those four!"

Mazzini exploded in his turn.

"Consumptive viper! That's what I called you, what I want to tell you! Ask him, ask the doctor who's to blame for your sons' meningitis: my father or your rotten lung? Yes, viper!"

They continued with increasing violence, until a moan from Bertita instantly sealed their lips. By one o'clock in the morning the child's light indigestion had disappeared, and, as it inevitably happens with all young married couples who have loved intensely, even for a while, they effected a reconciliation, all the more effusive for the infamy of the offenses.

A splendid day dawned, and as Berta arose she spit up blood. Her emotion and the terrible night were, without any doubt, primarily responsible. Mazzini held her in his embrace for a long while, and she cried hopelessly, but neither of them dared say a word.

At ten, they decided that after lunch they would go out. They were pressed for time so they ordered the servant to kill a hen.

The brilliant day had drawn the idiots from their bench. So while the servant was cutting off the head of the chicken in the kitchen, bleeding it parsimoniously (Berta had learned from her mother this effective method of conserving the freshness of meat), she thought she sensed something like breathing behind her. She turned and saw the four idiots, standing shoulder to shoulder, watching the operation with stupefaction. Red. . . . Red. . . .

"Señora! The boys are here in the kitchen."

Berta came in immediately; she never wanted them to set foot in the kitchen. Not even during these hours of full pardon, forgetfulness, and regained happiness could she avoid this horrible sight! Because, naturally, the more intense her raptures of love

54

for her husband and daughter, the greater her loathing for the monsters.

"Get them out of here, María! Throw them out! Throw them out, I tell you!"

The four poor little beasts, shaken and brutally shoved, went back to their bench.

After lunch, everyone went out; the servant to Buenos Aires and the couple and child for a walk among the country houses. They returned as the sun was sinking, but Berta wanted to talk for a while with her neighbors across the way. Her daughter quickly ran into the house.

In the meantime, the idiots had not moved from their bench the whole day. The sun had crossed the wall now, beginning to sink behind it, while they continued to stare at the bricks, more sluggish than ever.

Suddenly, something came between their line of vision and the wall. Their sister, tired of five hours with her parents, wanted to look around a bit on her own. She paused at the base of the wall and looked thoughtfully at its summit. She wanted to climb it; this could not be doubted. Finally she decided on a chair with the seat missing, but still she couldn't reach the top. Then she picked up a kerosene tin and, with a fine sense of relative space, placed it upright on the chair—with which she triumphed.

The four idiots, their gaze indifferent, watched how their sister succeeded patiently in gaining her equilibrium and how, on tip-toe, she rested her neck against the top of the wall between her straining hands. They watched her search everywhere for a toe hold to climb up higher.

The idiots' gaze became animated; the same insistent light fixed in all their pupils. Their eyes were fixed on their sister, as the growing sensation of bestial gluttony changed every line of their faces. Slowly they advanced toward the wall. The little girl, having succeeded in finding a toe hold and about to straddle the wall and surely fall off the other side, felt herself seized by one leg. Below her, the eight eyes staring into hers frightened her.

"Let loose! Let me go!" she cried, shaking her leg, but she was captive.

"Mama! Oh, Mama! Mama, Papa!" she cried imperiously. She tried still to cling to the top of the wall, but she felt herself pulled, and she fell.

"Mama, oh, Ma——" She could cry no more. One of the boys squeezed her neck, parting her curls as if they were feathers, and the other three dragged her by one leg toward the kitchen where that morning the chicken had been bled, holding her tightly, drawing the life out of her second by second.

Mazzini, in the house across the way, thought he heard his daughter's voice.

"I think she's calling you," he said to Berta.

They listened, uneasy, but heard nothing more. Even so, a moment later they said good-by, and, while Berta went to put up her hat, Mazzini went into the patio.

"Bertita!"

No one answered.

"Bertita!" He raised his already altered voice.

The silence was so funereal to his eternally terrified heart that a chill of horrible presentiment ran up his spine.

"My daughter, my daughter!" He ran frantically toward the back of the house. But as he passed by the kitchen he saw a sea of blood on the floor. He violently pushed open the half-closed door and uttered a cry of horror.

Berta, who had already started running when she heard Mazzini's anguished call, cried out, too. But as she rushed toward the kitchen, Mazzini, livid as death, stood in her way, holding her back.

"Don't go in! Don't go in!"

But Berta had seen the blood-covered floor. She could only utter a hoarse cry, throw her arms above her head and, leaning against her husband, sink slowly to the floor.

Drifting

The man stepped on something soft and yielding and immediately felt the bite on his foot. He leaped forward and, turning with an oath, saw a *yararacusú* coiled for another attack.

The man cast a quick glance at his foot, where two little drops of blood were slowly forming, and drew his machete from his belt. The snake saw the danger and drew its head deeper into the very center of its spiral, but the machete struck flat, smashing the snake's vertebrae.

The man bent over the bite, wiped off the drops of blood, and thought for a moment. A sharp pain originating in the two small violet punctures began to spread through his whole foot. Hurriedly he bound his ankle with his kerchief and continued along the trail to his small ranch.

The pain in his foot grew worse, with a sensation of swelling tautness, and suddenly the man felt two or three flashing pains radiating like lightning from the wound halfway up his calf. He moved his leg with difficulty now, and a metallic dryness in his throat, followed by a burning thirst, wrenched another oath from him.

He reached his ranch finally and threw his arms over the wheel of a sugar-cane press. The two violet puncture wounds had disappeared in the monstrous swelling of his foot. The skin seemed to be stretched thin and taut to the point of bursting. He tried to call his wife, but his voice broke from his parched throat in a raucous cry. Thirst devoured him.

"Dorotea!" he managed to gasp in a gravelly voice. "Get me some rum!"

His wife came running with a full glass, which the man gulped down in three swallows. But there was no taste at all.

"I told you rum, not water!" he grated again. "Get me rum!"

"But it is rum, Paulino!" the woman protested, frightened.

"No, you gave me water! I want rum, I tell you."

The woman ran away again, returning with the demijohn. The man drank two or three more glasses but felt nothing in his throat.

"Well, this is getting bad," he muttered, looking at his foot, livid and already bearing the luster of gangrene. The flesh swelled like a monstrous sausage over the buried binding of the kerchief.

The shooting pains were settling into continuous lightning-like flashes that now reached to his groin. The atrocious dryness in his throat that his breath seemed to heat to the boiling point increased by the second. When he tried to stand upright, a fulminating surge of vomit gripped him for half a minute, his head leaning against the wooden wheel.

But the man did not want to die, and he made his way down to the shore and climbed into his canoe. He seated himself in the stern and began to paddle into the middle of the Paraná. Once there, in the current of the river which runs about six miles an hour in the area of the Iguazú, he could reach Tacurú-Pacú in less than five hours.

The man, with somber energy, successfully reached the middle of the river, but there his numb hands dropped the paddle in the canoe, and after a new attack of vomiting—blood this time—he took a look at the sun, which had already crossed behind the mountain.

His entire leg, halfway up his thigh, was now a hard, misshapen slab of flesh bursting the seams of his pants. The man cut the binding and slit open his pants leg with his knife: the area of his groin was terribly painful, covered with huge livid spots, and puffed and swollen. The man thought he would never be able to reach Tacurú-Pacú by himself, and he decided to ask for help from his comrade Alves, even though they had been less than friendly with each other for some time.

The current of the river now rushed toward the Brazilian shore, and the man easily beached his canoe. He dragged himself along the trail up the slope, but after twenty meters, exhausted, he lay stretched out flat on his stomach.

"Alves!" he yelled with all the strength he could muster and listened in vain.

"Alves, comrade! Don't deny me this favor!" he shouted again, raising his head from the ground.

In the silence of the jungle there was not one sound. The man had the strength to return to his canoe, which the current seized again, carrying it swiftly downstream.

The Paraná there cuts through the depths of a great ravine whose walls, a hundred meters high, enclose the river in funereal shadow. From the shores, bordered by black blocks of basalt, ascends the forest, also black. Ahead, as well as upstream, the eternal lugubrious ramparts darken the whirling muddy river, ceaselessly boiling and bubbling. The landscape is menacing, and a deathlike silence reigns. At dusk, nevertheless, its somber and quiet beauty assumes a unique majesty.

The sun had already set when the man, half-conscious in the bottom of the canoe, was shaken by a violent chill. Suddenly, astonished, he dully raised his head; he felt better. His leg was less painful; his thirst was diminishing; and his chest, relieved now, relaxed in slow respiration.

The poison was beginning to subside, there was no question. He felt almost well, and, although he hadn't strength to move his hand, he was counting on the dewfall to restore him completely. He calculated he would be in Tacurú-Pacú in less than three hours.

His feeling of well-being increased and, with it, a somnolence filled with memories. He no longer had any feeling in his leg or in his belly. Would his comrade Gaona still be living in Tacurú-Pacú? Perhaps he might also see his former employer, Mister Dougald, and Mister Dougald's agent.

Would he be there soon? The sky to the west opened into a golden screen, and the river, too, took on color. A dusky freshness spilled from the mountain on the Paraguayan shore—in shadows now—a penetrating aroma of orange blossom and woodsy sweetness. High overhead a pair of macaws glided silently toward Paraguay.

The canoe drifted swiftly downstream on the golden river, whirling at times, caught in a gurgling whirlpool. The man in the canoe felt better every moment and meanwhile mused on the exact amount of time that had passed since he had last seen his employer, Mister Dougald. Three years? Maybe not, not that long. Two years and nine months? Perhaps. Eight and a half months. Yes, that was it, surely.

Suddenly he felt freezing cold up to his chest. What could it be? And his breathing, too . . .

He had met the man who bought Mister Dougald's timber, Lorenzo Cubilla, in Puerto Esperanza on a Good Friday . . . Friday? Yes, or Thursday . . .

The man slowly stretched the fingers of his hand.

"A Thursday . . ."

And he stopped breathing.

Acosta, the steward of the *Meteor*, the ship that steamed every two weeks up the Upper Paraná, knew one thing very well, and it was this: nothing is as swift, not even the river itself, as the explosion caused by a demijohn of *caña* among thirsty workers on a work site. His adventure with Korner, then, took place in a territory he knew very well.

By absolute rule—with only one exception—the law on the Upper Paraná does not permit *caña* at a work camp. The company stores don't sell it, nor is a single bottle tolerated, whatever its origin. At the work camps, there are resentments and bitter feelings it is best not to recall to the *mensú*, the contracted workers. One hundred grams of alcohol per man would, even after only two hours, result in a completely militant camp.

An explosion of such magnitude was contrary to Acosta's own interests, and for this reason he exercised his ingenuity in acts of minor contraband, drinks issued to the workers on the ship itself as the workers debarked at each port. The captain knew it, as well as all the passengers, composed almost exclusively of owners and foremen of the work camps. But as the astute trafficker never administered more than a prudent amount, everything went along very well.

Well, one day misfortune dictated that at the insistence of a particularly boisterous group of peons, Acosta relaxed slightly his usually rigid prudence. The result was uproarious good nature, so merry that the workers' trunks and guitars were flying through the air as they debarked.

The scandal was serious. The captain and almost all the passengers descended from the ship, feeling that a new "dance" was necessary, but this time the dance of the whip on the wildest heads. This procedure is customary, and the captain had a swift and sure arm. The storm ceased immediately. Even so, the captain ordered one of the more rebellious of the *mensú* tied by the foot to the mainmast, and everything returned to normal.

But now it was Acosta's turn. The owner of the work camp in whose port the steamship was docked accosted the steward: "You and you alone are responsible for this situation: for ten miserable centavos, you spoil the peons and cause this row!"

The steward, being a mestizo, temporized.

"Shut up! You should be ashamed!" Korner continued. "For ten miserable centavos! I promise you that as soon as we reach Posadas, I'm going to report this trickery to Mitain!"

Mitain owned the *Meteor*, which failed to impress Acosta in the least. Finally, he lost patience.

"When you come right down to it," he responded, "you don't have anything to do with this. If you don't like it, complain to anyone you want. In my office, I do whatever *I* want."

"We'll see about that!" shouted Korner, preparing to go on board. But as he was going up the ladder he saw over the bronze handrail the worker tied to the mainmast. Whether or not there was irony in the prisoner's eyes, Korner was convinced there was, and he recognized in the dark little Indian with the cold eyes and pointed mustache a peon he had had some trouble with three months before.

He walked to the mainmast, rage turning his face even redder. The worker, still smiling, watched him approach.

"So it's you!" Korner said. "Everywhere I go, I find *you* in my way! I've forbidden you to set foot in my work camp, and yet that's where you've just been . . . , *buddy*!"

The worker, as if he hadn't heard, continued to look at him with his little smile. Then Korner, blind with rage, struck him in the face, first the left side, then the right.

"Take that . . . buddy! That's the only way to treat *friends* like you!"

The *mensú* turned livid and stared at Korner, who heard this word: "Someday . . . !"

Korner felt a new impulse, to make the worker swallow his

threat, but he managed to contain himself and went on board, hurling invectives against the steward who had brought this hell to the work camp.

But this time it was Acosta's turn to take the offensive. What was the worst thing he could do to this Korner of the red face and the sharp tongue, and to his damned work site?

It didn't take him long to find the answer. On the very next trip upriver, he was very careful to provide surreptitiously one or two demijohns of *caña* to the peons debarking in Puerto Profundidad (Korner's port). These *mensú*, even louder than most, hid the contraband *caña* in their trunks, and that very night trouble erupted at the work camp.

For two months every ship descending the river after the *Meteor* had gone up invariably picked up four or five wounded men in Puerto Profundidad. Korner, desperate, could not localize the incendiary, the supplier of the contraband *caña*. But after a time Acosta considered it discreet not to feed the fires anymore, and there was no more machete swinging in the camp. A neat piece of business, after all, for the trafficker who had conceived and won vengeance, especially considering it was on Korner's bald head.

Two years passed. The *mensú* who had been slapped in the face had worked at various work sites but had never been permitted to set foot in Puerto Profundidad. Because of the old dispute with Korner and the episode at the mainmast, the Indian had become non grata to the management. The *mensú*, in the meantime, overcome by his native laziness, spent long idle periods of time in Posadas, living by the pointed mustache that inflamed the hearts of the female *mensualeras*. His manelike head of hair, a fashion uncommon in the extreme north, enchanted the girls who were seduced by the oil and the violently scented lotions.

One fine day the *mensú* decided to accept the first contract that came his way, and again he went up the Paraná. He had soon cancelled out his advance, but he had a magnificent strength; he tried one port after another, hoping to get where he really wanted to go. But it was in vain. In every camp they accepted him gladly, except in Profundidad: there, he wasn't needed. Then he was seized by a new attack of lassitude and exhaustion, and he again spent several months in Posadas, his body enervated and his mustache saturated with essences.

Three more years went by. During this period the worker went up the Upper Paraná only one time, having finally concluded that his current means of livelihood was much less fatiguing than jobs upriver. And, although the former extreme exhaustion of his arms was now replaced by constant fatigue in his legs, he found that to his pleasure.

He did not know, or at least he did not frequent, any part of Posadas except Bajada and the port. He never left the workers' district; he went from one woman worker's shack to another, then to the tavern, then to the port to celebrate the chorus of shouting at the daily embarkation of the contract workers; then night would find him at the five-centavos-a-dance dance halls.

"Eh, amigo!" the peons would shout to him. "You don't like your hatchet anymore! You like that dancing girl, eh, amigo!"

The Indian would smile, satisfied with his mustache and his shining hair.

One day, nevertheless, he perked up his ears alertly when he heard some labor contractors offering splendid advance salaries to a group of recently debarked contract workers. They were making the offer for a leased site at Puerto Cabriuva, almost at the falls of Guayrá, next to Korner's establishment. There was much wood in the barranca there, and they needed men. Good daily pay, and a little *caña*, of course.

Three days later, the same contract workers who had just returned exhausted from nine months' hard labor again boarded ship, after having debauched fantastically and brutally their two hundred pesos of advance pay in forty-eight hours.

These peons were not a little surprised to see the "pretty boy" amongst them.

"Eh, amigo, where's the party!" they yelled at him. "So it's the hatchet again, is it?"

They reached Puerto Cabriuva, and that very afternoon this crew was assigned to the rafts.

Subsequently, they spent two months working beneath a burning sun, moving huge trees from the barranca down to the river, using levers, in backbreaking efforts that stretched the neck tendons of the seven workers taut as wire.

Then came the work in the river: swimming, twenty fathoms of water beneath them, towing the trees, lining them up, immobilized in the branches of the treetops for hours on end, with only their heads and arms above the water. After four to six hours, the men would climb back on the raft or, to be more accurate, would be hoisted onto it, since they would be frozen from the cold water. It isn't strange, then, that the manager would always keep back a little *caña* for such occasions, the only times when the law was infringed upon. The men would take a drink and return again to the water.

Our *mensú*, then, played his part in this rough business and then descended the river to Puerto Profundidad on the enormous log raft. Our man had counted on this fact so he could get off at that port. In fact, in the work-site office, they either did not recognize him or they had been blind to his identity because of the urgency of the job. What is certain is that, once the raft was secured, they commended to the *mensú*, along with three other peons, the job of driving a herd of mules to Carrería, several miles farther inland. That was all the *mensú* wanted, and he left the following morning, driving his little herd along the main road.

It was very hot that day. Between the two walls of the forest, the red dirt road was dazzlingly bright. The silence of the jungle at that hour seemed to augment the dizzying shimmer of air over the volcanic sand. Not a breath of air, not a cheep from a bird. Beneath the leaden sun that had silenced even the cicadas, the herd, crowned by an aureole of horseflies, advanced monotonously along the road, heads hanging low from drowsiness and the burning light.

At one o'clock the peons stopped to prepare maté tea. A moment later they spied their *patrón* coming toward them along the road. He was alone, on horseback, wearing a large pith helmet. Korner stopped, asked the peon closest to him two or three questions, and then recognized the Indian, stooped over the water kettle.

Korner's sweaty red face turned a shade darker, and he rose in his stirrups.

"Hey, you! What are you doing here?" he shouted, furious.

Unhurriedly, the Indian rose to his feet.

"You don't seem to know how to speak to a man," he answered, walking toward his *patrón*.

Korner pulled out his revolver and fired but missed. The upward swing of a machete had tossed the revolver into the air, the index finger still gripping the trigger. An instant later Korner was on the ground, the Indian on top of him.

The peons had stood by frozen, obviously stunned by their companion's audacity.

"Go on," he shouted to them in a choked voice, not turning his head. The others continued with their duty, which was driving the mules as they had been ordered, and the herd disappeared down the road.

The *mensú*, then, still holding Korner against the ground, tossed the man's knife aside and leapt to his feet. In his hand he held his *patrón*'s elk leather whip.

"Get up!" he said.

Korner rose, bleeding and babbling insults, and lunged toward the *mensú*. But the whip struck his face with such force that he fell to the ground.

"Get up," the worker repeated.

Again, Korner got to his feet.

"Now, get going."

And as Korner, maddened by indignation, again lunged toward the Indian, the whip fell across his back with a dry and terrible thud.

"Get going."

Korner walked. He was humiliated, almost apoplectic, and his bleeding hand and fatigue had overcome him, yet he walked. At times, nevertheless, he stopped and shouted a storm of threats, overcome by the magnitude of the affront. The worker seemed not to hear. Only again the terrible whip fell across Korner's shoulders.

"Get going."

They were alone on the road, walking toward the river, both silent, the *mensú* a little behind Korner. The sun burned down on their heads, their boots, their feet. There was the same silence as there had been that morning, filtered through the same vague buzzing of a lethargic jungle. The only sound, the occasional crack of the whip on Korner's back.

"Get going."

For five hours, kilometer after kilometer, Korner sipped to the dregs the humiliation and pain of his situation. Wounded, choking from momentary surges of apoplexy, several times he attempted to stop. In vain. The *mensú* said not a word, but the whip fell again, and Korner walked.

Since the sun was setting, and in order to avoid the work-camp office, they abandoned the main road for a path that also led to the Paraná. With this change Korner lost his last hope for help, and he fell to the ground, determined not to walk a step farther. But the whip, wielded by an arm accustomed to the hatchet, began to fall.

"Get going."

At the fifth whiplash, Korner arose, and during the final quarter hour the blows fell untiringly every twenty steps upon the back and head of Korner, who was staggering like a sleepwalker.

Finally they reached the river and walked along the shore until they came to the raft. Korner was forced to climb upon it, walk, as well as he could, to the farthest extreme, and there, at the end of his strength, he fell face down, his head between his arms.

The *mensú* approached.

"Now," he said, "this is so you'll learn to speak to a person properly. And this is for slapping people in the face." And the whip, with terrible and monotonous violence, fell unceasingly on Korner's back, carving out bloody strips of hair and flesh.

Korner lay motionless. Then the *mensú* cut the ties of the raft and climbed into a wooden boat. He tied one end of the rope to the stern and then poled vigorously.

As slight as was the tug upon the enormous craft of tree trunks, the first effort sufficed. Imperceptibly the raft eddied out into the current, and the *mensú* cut the rope free.

The sun had gone down. The atmosphere, stifling two hours before, was now funereally quiet and cool. Beneath the still green sky, the raft, spinning, drifted downstream, entered the transparent shadow of the Paraguayan coast, and emerged again, now only a dot in the distance.

The worker also floated downstream, but obliquely, toward Brazil, where he would remain to the end of his days.

"I'm going to miss the old gang," he murmured, as he bound a rag around his exhausted wrist. And with a cold glance at the raft, moving toward inevitable disaster, he concluded, under his breath, "But *he'll* never slap anyone in the face again, the damned gringo!"

In the Middle of the Night

One day during flood season I found myself being carried by the full and foaming waters of the Upper Paraná from San Ignacio toward the sugar mill at San Juan on a current that was six miles wide in the channel and nine across the shoals.

Since April, I had been waiting for the flood. My roaming in a canoe up and down the Paraná at low water had finally wearied the Greek. The Greek is an old sailor from the English navy who had probably before that been a pirate on the Aegean, his native sea, and who, more certainly, had been a brandy smuggler in San Ignacio for more than fifteen years. This was my river master.

"All right," he said to me when he saw the swollen river. "You can pass now for half a sailor, half a regular sailor. But there's still something you don't know, and that's the Paraná when it's flooded." He pointed, "You see those rocks above the El Greco millstone? Well, when the water reaches that point and you can't see any of the rocks on the shoals, then you can boast about having navigated the Teyucuaré and feel you're worth something when you get back. Take along an extra paddle; you're sure to break one or two. And get one of those thousand tins of kerosene from your house and seal it well with wax. Even so, you may very well drown."

And so, calmly, I was letting myself be carried toward the Teyucuaré but with an extra paddle because of the Greek's advice.

At least half the tree trunks, rotten straw, scum, and dead animals that come downriver in a great flood get trapped in the deep backwater of the Teyucuaré. There they await the coming of the high water; they appear to be solid ground, edging up on the banks, slipping along the shoreline like a piece of land broken loose. That whole backwater is actually a Sargasso sea.

Little by little, as they drift in wider and wider circles, the tree trunks are caught in the current and tumble downstream, whirling and dipping, finally plunging and somersaulting along the final rock shoals of the Teyucuaré where cliffs rise eighty meters on both sides.

These cliff faces enclose the river perpendicularly, narrowing its channel to a third its former width. Then the Paraná joins these waters, seeking an exit, forming a series of rapids almost unnavigable even in low water unless the boatman is unusually alert. Neither is there any way to avoid the rapids since the central current of the river precipitates itself through the narrows formed by the cliffs, widening into a tumultuous curve pouring into the lower pool defined by a steady line of foam.

Now it was my turn to ride with the current. I sped like a breeze over the rapids and was caught in the churning waters of the channel that dragged me first stern-first, then bow-first. I had to be extremely judicious in my use of the paddle, digging on first one side and then the other to maintain equilibrium, since my canoe was only sixty centimeters across, weighed some thirty kilos, and had a skin of only two millimeters at the thickest point. A good hard rap of the knuckles could seriously damage it. But offsetting these drawbacks, it achieved a fantastic maneuverability that had allowed me to forge my way up and down the river, from south to north and east to west, never, of course, forgetting for a moment my craft's instability.

Finally, always downstream amidst sticks and seeds that seemed as motionless as I, although we were rolling swiftly downstream on smooth water, I passed the island of Toro, left behind the mouth of the Yabebirí and the port of Santa Ana, paddled up the Yabebirí to the sugar mill, where I immediately returned to the Paraná since I wanted to reach San Ignacio the same evening.

But back in Santa Ana I stopped, hesitant. The Greek was right: the Paraná at low water or normal flow is one thing, but these swollen waters were something quite different. Even in my canoe, the rapids I had passed as I returned upriver had worried me, not for the strength needed to paddle against the current, but because of the fear of overturning. Every shoal, as everyone knows, forms an adjacent pool of still water: this is precisely where the danger lies—in coming out of dead water to collide, sometimes at right angles, with a current going like hell. If one's craft is stable, there's nothing to fear; but, with mine, nothing is simpler than sounding the rapids upside down if the light is at all bad. So, since it was beginning to get dark, I was in the process of beaching my canoe to wait for the following day when I saw a man and a woman approaching me down the barranca.

They looked to be man and wife, foreigners, I would judge from their appearance, although familiar with the clothing of the country. He was wearing a shirt with the sleeves rolled to the elbow, though it showed no signs of hard work. She was wearing a one-piece apronlike garment cinched by an oilcloth belt. Upstanding members of the bourgeoisie, in short: their air of satisfaction and well-being was typical of that class, qualities assured at the expense of the work of others.

Both, after a cordial greeting, examined my toylike canoe with great curiosity and then looked at the river.

"You do well, sir, to stay here," the man said. "With the river like this, it's no place to be in the middle of the night."

The woman adjusted her belt. "Oh, sometimes," she smiled, coquettishly.

"Naturally," he replied. "I didn't mean that in regard to us. I was referring to this gentleman here."

And he said to me, "If you're thinking of staying here, sir, we can offer you a comfortable evening. We've had a little business here for the past two years. It's not very much, but one does what he can. Isn't that right, sir?"

I nodded agreeably, following them to their little store, since a store was really what it was. I dined, nevertheless, much better than in my own house, attended to with details of comfort that seemed a dream in a place like that. These were excellent types, my bourgeois, happy and clean—after all, they did no hard work.

After an excellent cup of coffee, they returned with me to the beach where I pulled my canoe even higher, knowing that the Paraná, once its waters run red and are pocked with whirlpools, is capable of rising two meters in one night. Again they both contemplated the invisible mass of the river.

"Yes, you do very well to stay, sir," the man repeated. "No one can navigate the Teyucuaré at night, not like it is now. There's no one capable of that . . . , except my wife."

I turned abruptly toward the woman who was again toying with her belt.

"You've passed the Teyucuaré in the middle of the night?" I asked.

"Oh, yes sir! But only once . . . and not because I wanted to. We were crazy that night."

"But the *river*?" I insisted.

"The river," the man interrupted. "It was crazy, too. You know those reefs around the island of Toro, don't you? They're half out of water now. But that night they were completely covered. Everything was water as far as you could see, and water roaring over the rocks; we heard it from here. That was some night, sir. And I have a little souvenir of that night. Would you strike a match, please?"

The man raised his pants leg to the back of his knee, and on the inner side of his calf I saw a deep scar, crisscrossed with thick silvery scars like a map.

"You see that, sir? That's my souvenir of that night. The sting of a ray. . . ."

Then I recalled a story I'd heard somewhere about a woman who had rowed one whole day and night, carrying her dying husband. And *this* was the woman, this neat little bourgeois woman, delighted with success?

"Yes, sir, *I'm* the one," she burst out laughing at my astonished expression—no words were needed. "But now I'd die a hundred times before I'd ever think of attempting it. Times were different then; that's all over now!"

"Forever," the man seconded. "When I recall . . . We were

mad, sir. But we were spurred on by misery and disillusion. Yes, those were different times!"

I could believe it! If they had done that, times must have been different. But I didn't want to go to bed without learning some of the details, and there in the darkness facing the same river, invisible except for the warm water touching the shore at our feet—but audible, rising and rising as far as the opposite shore—I came to know what a feat that nocturnal epic had been.

Deceived about the resources of the country, having exhausted what little capital they had brought with them in mistakes common to new settlers, the couple found themselves one day at the end of their resources. But they were courageous, and they used their last pesos to buy a useless old boat which they rebuilt at the cost of infinite fatigue, and then with it they undertook the river traffic, buying honey, oranges, bamboo, straw—all on a small scale—from the settlers scattered along the river, and then sold on the beach of Posadas, almost always making bad deals, since they were at first ignorant of the pulse of the market. They carried liters of *caña* brandy when barrels of it had been delivered the day before, and oranges when the coast was yellow with them.

A hard life and daily failure had erased from their minds any preoccupation except that of arriving at Posadas by dawn and then rowing back up the Paraná by the strength of their arms. The woman always accompanied her husband, rowing with him.

On one such day, the twenty-third of December, the woman said, "We could take our tobacco to Posadas and the bananas from Francescué. On the return we could bring Christmas cakes and colored candles. Day after tomorrow is Christmas, and we can easily sell them to the little stores."

The man replied, "We won't sell many in Santa Ana, but we can sell the rest in San Ignacio."

So that same afternoon they descended the river to Posadas, to row back up the following day before dawn.

Well: the Paraná was swollen with dirty flood waters rising by the minute. And when the tropical rains had simultaneously emptied all their waters into the river basin upstream, the long sections of quiet water which are the rower's most faithful friend were inundated. Water poured down from every direction. At such times the immense volume of the river becomes a single liquid mass flowing uninterruptedly. And if at a distance the channel of the river looks like a smooth ribbon with straight luminous stripes, when one is close at hand, upon the river, the whirling eddies form a surface like moiré silk.

Nevertheless, this couple did not hesitate an instant to begin rowing sixty kilometers upriver, their only motivation that of earning a few pesos. Their inborn love of the centavo had been exacerbated by glimpsed poverty, and even though they were now near their golden dream—a dream later realized—at that moment they would have confronted the Amazon itself had it meant augmenting their savings by five pesos.

So they undertook the return trip, the woman rowing and the man poling in the stern. They scarcely moved, although they threw all their strength into the rowing, strength that had to be redoubled every twenty minutes when they came to the rapids, where the woman's oars splashed with desperate intensity and the man's effort doubled him over the pole buried a meter deep in water.

So passed ten, fifteen hours. Brushing the trees and reeds along the shore, imperceptibly the boat ascended the immense and shining avenue of water and, close to the shore, seemed a very poor thing indeed.

The couple was in perfect training, and they were not oarsmen to be defeated by fourteen or sixteen hours of rowing. But it was when they were within sight of Santa Ana, preparing to come ashore to spend the night, that the man stepped out into the mud, screamed an oath, and leaped back into the boat: above his heel, on the Achilles tendon, a blackened puncture wound with livid, already swollen edges announced the sting of the ray.

The woman smothered a cry.

"What was it . . . ? A ray?"

The man had clasped his foot in his hands, squeezing it with convulsive force.

"Yes."

"Is it very painful?" she added, seeing his grimace. And he, his teeth clenched, "Like a thousand demons . . ."

During the harsh struggle that had hardened their hands and features, the couple had eliminated from their conversation any words that taxed their energies. Wildly, each tried to think of a remedy. What? They could think of nothing. Suddenly the woman remembered: applications of dried chili plant.

"Quick, Andrés!" she exclaimed, grabbing the oars. "Lie down in the stern; I'll row to Santa Ana."

As the man, his hand still clutching his ankle, lay down in the stern, the woman began to row.

For three hours she rowed in silence, concentrating her dark anguish in desperate muteness, erasing from her mind anything that might rob her of strength. In the stern, the man, in turn, was immersed in his torture, since there is nothing comparable to the hideous pain caused by the sting of a ray (if one excludes the scraping of a tubercular bone). Only occasionally did a groan escape that, in spite of his efforts, was drawn out into a scream. But the woman didn't hear, or tried not to hear; her only sign of conscious awareness was her glances over her shoulder to gauge the remaining distance.

Finally they arrived at Santa Ana, but none of the settlers had the necessary chili plant. What to do? Not even in the wildest dream was there any possibility of reaching the town. In the depths of her anxiety the woman suddenly recalled that up the Teyucuaré, at the foot of Blosset's banana grove, on the water itself, lived a German naturalist working for the Paris Museum. She remembered, too, that he had cured two neighbors of snake-bite and was more than likely capable of curing her husband.

So she resumed the trek, commencing the most vigorous struggle ever undertaken by a simple human being—a woman!—against the implacable will of Nature.

Everything was against her: the rising river and the distorted images of the night that tricked her into believing the boat was close to shore when in reality she was exhausting herself in the midst of a current ten fathoms deep, her hands staining the oar grip with blood and running blisters; they were in the power of the river, the night . . . and misery.

She was able to save some strength as far as the mouth of the Yabebirí, but, in the interminable broad waters from the Yabe-birí to the first steeply rising cliffs of the Teyucuaré, there was no relief because outside the normal channel the river ran through beds of water plants and every three strokes of the oar plowed up plants instead of water; the bow of the boat caught in the knotty stems, dragging them along behind, and the woman had to reach into the water and tear them loose. When she would drop again, exhausted, onto the wooden seat, her body, from her head to her feet, was one mass of suffering.

Finally, as the night sky to the north was blackened by the hills of the Teyucuaré, the man, who had some time ago abandoned his grasp on his ankle in order to hold desperately to the sides of the boat, screamed.

The woman stopped rowing.

"Does it hurt much?"

He was surprised by her voice. "Yes," he panted. "But I didn't mean to scream. I couldn't help it." And he added more quietly, as if he feared he would sob if he raised his voice, "I won't let it happen again. . . ."

He knew very well what it would mean in those circumstances to lose spirit in front of his poor wife, who was accomplishing the impossible. There is no doubt that the shout had escaped him because the hideous pain in his foot and his ankle, the exacerbating, flashing, stabbing pain, had maddened him.

But now they were in the shadow of the first cliff, striking the brute mass rising sharply some hundred meters overhead with the port oar. From there to the shoals south of the Teyucuaré the water was still and calm in some sections—an enormous relief the woman could not enjoy because another scream arose from the stern. She did not look at him. But the wounded man, bathed

82

in cold sweat, trembling to the fingers gripping the sides of the boat, could no longer contain himself, and again he screamed.

For a long while the husband had conserved a residue of energy, of courage, out of compassion for that other human suffering, for the woman exhausting her last forces, and only at long intervals had he allowed a moan to escape. But finally all his resistance was reduced to a pap of shattered nerves, and, crazy with pain, unaware of it himself, he had burst out in uninterrupted screams of intolerable suffering.

Meanwhile, the woman, bent double, kept her eyes fixed on the shore to hold the boat at the correct distance from the shore. She didn't think; she didn't hear; she didn't feel: she rowed. Only when a stronger scream, a true howl of torture, shattered the night would she loosen her grip on the oars.

But finally she let go of the oars completely and threw her arms across the gunwales.

"Don't scream," she murmured.

"I can't help it!" he cried. "It's too much!"

She sobbed, "I know . . . ! I understand! But don't scream. I can't row when you scream!"

"I understand that, but I can't help it. Ohhhhh!" And, maddened by pain, he screamed louder and louder, "I can't help it! I can't help it! I can't . . ."

The woman sat a long while, her head on her arms, crushed, motionless, dead. Finally, once again, she sat upright and mutely resumed the trek.

What that woman did then, that same small woman who had already rowed eighteen hours with a dying husband in the bottom of the boat, was one of those things that happens only once in a lifetime. She had to confront the rapids south of the Teyucuaré in the shadow of night, rapids that thrust her ten times into the whirlpools of the channel. Another ten times she tried to hug the cliff and drag the boat around the bend, and failed. She turned again to the rapids, where finally she succeeded in finding the correct angle of entry and then was caught in the power of those waters for thirty-five minutes, rowing desperately so as not to lose headway. She rowed all that time with her eyes smarting from blinding sweat, without releasing her hold a single instant. For thirty-five minutes she stared at the cliff three meters away she could not get around, gaining only centimeters every five minutes, where the water flowed so swiftly she had the sensation she was beating her oars against the air.

With what strength—her strength was exhausted—with what incredible straining of her last vital forces was she able to sustain that nightmarish struggle? She, more than anyone, would never be able to say. Especially when one realizes that, as a stimulus, the pitiable woman had only the measured screams of the husband lying in the stern.

The rest of the trip—two more rapids in the depths of the abyss and a last, but infinitely long, rapid as she turned the bend of the last hill—demanded no greater effort. But when the boat finally touched the shore of the port of Blosset and the woman tried to get out of the boat to make it secure, she suddenly found she had no arms, no legs, no head—she could feel nothing except the hill tumbling down upon her . . . , and she fainted.

"That was how it was, sir. I was in bed two months, and you already saw what my leg looks like. Ah, the pain, sir. But if it weren't for this woman here I'd never have been able to tell you the story," he concluded, placing his hand on his wife's shoulder.

The small woman accepted his gesture, laughing. Both of them smiled, calm, clean, established at last in their lucrative store—their ideal.

And as we stood again looking at the dark, warm, rising river flowing by, I asked myself what ideal is to be found at the core of an action when it is separated from the motivations that have fired it, since my wretched merchants, unbeknown to themselves, had committed an act of heroism.

Juan Darién

Herein is told the tale of a tiger who was raised and educated among men and whose name was Juan Darién. Dressed in pants and a shirt he attended school for four years, and he did his lessons correctly even though he was a tiger from the jungle; this was possible because his body was that of a human being, in accordance with what is told in the following lines.

Once upon a time, at the beginning of autumn, a plague of smallpox that killed many people was visited upon a small village in a distant land. Brothers lost their little sisters, and infants who were just learning to walk were left with neither father nor mother. Mothers in turn lost their children, and one poor young widow woman herself carried her baby boy to be buried, the only thing she had in the world. When she returned to her home, she sat thinking about her child. And she murmured, "God should have had more compassion for me, but he has taken away my son. There may be angels in heaven, but my son doesn't know them. My poor little baby! I'm the only person he ever knew."

Since she was sitting behind her house, facing a little gate, she could see the jungle as she gazed into the distance.

Well now, in that jungle there were many ferocious animals that roared at nightfall and at dawn. And the poor woman, still sitting there, chanced to see in the darkness a tiny, hesitant creature coming through her gate, something that looked like a little cat with scarcely strength to walk. The woman bent down and picked up a little tiger, only a few days old, its eyes still unopened. And when the miserable little cub felt the touch of her hands, it purred with contentment because it was no longer alone. The woman held the little enemy of man at arm's length for a

87

long while, the small defenseless beast she could so easily have destroyed. But she stood pensively considering the helpless cub that had come from heaven knows where and whose mother was surely dead. Without thinking what she was doing she held the cub to her bosom and encircled him with her large hands. And the little tiger, feeling the warmth, sought a comfortable position, purred tranquilly, and fell asleep with his head pressed fast against the maternal breast.

The woman, still pensive, entered the house. And for the remainder of the night, hearing the cub's whimpers of hunger and seeing his unopened eyes and how he sought her breast, she felt in her aching heart that in the supreme law of the Universe one life equals another. . . .

And so she suckled the little tiger.

The cub was saved, and the mother had found enormous consolation. So great was this consolation that she considered with terror the moment when he would be taken from her forcibly, because if it came to be known in the village that she was suckling a wild thing they would surely kill the little creature. What should she do? The cub—soft and affectionate as he played at her breast—was now her own son.

So these were the circumstances when one rainy night a man running by the woman's house heard the gruff wail that startles a human being even when it comes from a newly born beast. The man stopped abruptly and knocked on the door while he groped for his revolver. The mother had heard the steps, and, wild with anxiety, she ran to hide the little tiger in the garden. But such was her good fortune that, as she tried to open the back door, she found herself standing before a gentle, wise old serpent who was barring her way. The hapless woman was about to scream with terror when the serpent spoke.

"Do not fear, woman," it said to her. "Your mother's heart led you to save a life from the Universe where all lives have the same value. But men will not understand you, and they will wish to kill your new son. Never fear; go in peace. From this moment your son will have human form; he will never be recognized as a beast. Shape his heart; teach him to be good, as you are, and he will never know he is not a man. Unless . . . unless a mother among men shall accuse him; unless a mother demands that he pay with his blood what you have given to him, your son will always be worthy of you. Go in peace, mother, and hurry; the man is breaking down your door."

And the woman believed the serpent, because in all man's religions the serpent knows the mysteries of the lives of those who people the world. So she ran to open the door, and the enraged man with a revolver in his hand entered and searched through the house without finding anything. When he left, the mother tremblingly opened her rebozo where she had hidden the little tiger in her bosom, and in the place of the cub she saw a baby boy sleeping peacefully. Overcome with happiness, she cried silently a long while over her savage son suddenly become a human, tears of gratitude that twelve years later the same boy would repay in blood on her grave.

Time passed. The new boy needed a name: she called him Juan Darién. He needed food, clothes, and shoes: she worked night and day to provide for all his needs. She was still very young, and she could have married again if she had wished, but her son's deep love sufficed, a love she returned with all her heart.

Juan Darién was truly worthy of being loved; he was noble, good, and generous like no other. For his mother, particularly, he had profound veneration. He never lied. (Perhaps because at heart he was a wild being? It is possible, since it is still not known what effect purity of soul imbibed at the breast of a saintly woman may have on a newly born animal.)

This was Juan Darién. And he went to school with children of his age who often teased him because of his shyness and his coarse hair. Juan Darién was not extremely intelligent, but he compensated for this by his great love for study.

So things went, but, when the child was not quite ten years old, his mother died. Juan Darién suffered more than can be told, until time finally softened his pain. But from that time forward he was a sad child whose only desire was to instruct himself.

Now there is something we must confess: Juan Darién was not loved in the village. People in isolated jungle villages do not like boys who are too generous and who study with all their hearts. He was, besides, the best pupil in the school. And this situation precipitated the denouement of our story with an event that confirmed the serpent's prophecy.

The village was preparing to celebrate a great festival, and the people had ordered fireworks from a distant city. Since an inspector was coming to observe the classes, the school children were being given a general review. When the inspector arrived, the schoolmaster had him question the best pupil of all: Juan Darién. Juan was the student who always excelled, but in the emotion of the moment, he stammered and a strange sound tied his tongue.

The inspector observed the pupil a long while, then spoke in a low voice to the schoolmaster.

"Who is that boy? Where did he come from?"

"His name is Juan Darién," the schoolmaster replied, "and he was raised by a woman who is dead now, but no one knows where he came from."

"Very strange, very strange," the inspector murmured, observing the coarse hair and the greenish reflection in Juan Darién's eyes when he stood in the shadows.

The inspector knew that there are stranger things in the world than any man can invent, and at the same time he knew that simply by asking Juan Darién questions he would never be able to find out if the pupil had once been what he feared: a wild animal. But as there are men who in special states remember things that have happened to their grandfathers, it was also possible that under hypnotic suggestion Juan Darién might remember his life as a savage beast. And children who read this and don't know what that means can ask some grown-up persons about it.

For this purpose, then, the inspector stepped upon the platform and spoke as follows: "Well, children. Now I want one of you to describe the jungle for us. You have been brought up almost in the jungle and you know it well. What is the jungle like? What happens in it? This is what I want to know. Let's see, you," he added, pointing at random to a pupil. "Come up to the platform and tell us what you have seen."

The child went up, and, although he was frightened, he talked for a while. He said that there are gigantic trees in the forest and climbing vines and little flowers. When he concluded, another child went to the platform, and then another. And, although they all knew the jungle very well, they responded in the same way, because children, and many adults, do not tell what they have *seen* but what they have *read* about what they have seen. And finally the inspector said, "Now it's Juan Darién's turn."

Juan Darién said more or less what the others had said. But the inspector, placing his hand on his shoulder, exclaimed, "No, no. I want you to remember exactly what you have seen. Close your eyes."

Juan Darién closed his eyes.

"Good," the inspector continued. "Tell me what you see in the jungle."

Juan Darién, his eyes still closed, hesitated a moment before answering.

"I don't see anything," he said finally.

"Soon you will see. Let's pretend it's three o'clock in the morning, a little before dawn. We have just eaten, let's say. We are in the jungle . . . in the dark. . . . In front of us there is a small stream. What do you see?"

For a moment Juan Darién was silent. And in the classroom and in the nearby jungle there was also a great silence. Suddenly Juan Darién shivered, and in a slow voice, as if he were dreaming, he said, "I see rocks going by, and bending branches. . . . And the ground. . . . And I see dry leaves flattened on the rocks. . . ."

"One moment!" the inspector interrupted him. "The rocks and the leaves going by, how high are they?"

The inspector asked this because if Juan Darién were truly "seeing" what he had been doing in the jungle as a wild animal going to drink after eating, he would also see that a crouching tiger or panther, as he approaches the river, sees the rocks at eye

91

level. And he repeated, "How high are the rocks?"

And Juan Darién, still with his eyes closed, replied, "They are on the ground. . . . They graze your ears. . . . And the loose leaves move with your breath. . . . And I feel the dampness of mud on my . . ."

Juan Darién's voice stopped short.

"Where?" the inspector asked in a firm voice. "Where do you feel the dampness?"

"On my whiskers," Juan Darién said in a hoarse voice, opening his eyes, frightened.

Dusk was falling, and through the window one could see nearby the already gloomy jungle. The students didn't understand how terrible that revelation had been, but neither did they laugh about the extraordinary whiskers of Juan Darién, who had no whiskers at all. They didn't laugh, because the child's face was pale and anxious.

Class was over. The inspector was not an evil man, but, like all men who live very close to the jungle, he had a blind hatred of tigers, which was why he confided to the schoolmaster in a low voice:

"Juan Darién must be killed. He is a beast of the jungle, possibly a tiger. We must kill him because if we don't, sooner or later he will kill all of us. Up till now his beast's wickedness has not been awakened, but it will explode some day, and then he will devour us all if we allow him to live among us. We must, then, kill him. The difficulty is that we can't do it as long as he has human form, because we cannot prove that he is a tiger. He looks like a man, and with men one must proceed with caution. I know there is a wild animal tamer in the city. Let us send for him, and he will find a way to make Juan Darién return to his tiger's body. And even if he can't convert him into a tiger, people will believe us and cast him into the jungle. Let us send for the tamer immediately before Juan Darién escapes."

But the last thing Juan Darién was thinking of was escape, because he was not aware that anything was happening at all. How could he doubt he was a man when he had never felt anything but love for other people and didn't even hate harmful animals?

But the word was spreading from mouth to mouth and Juan Darién began to suffer its effect. People didn't answer when he spoke to them; they withdrew hastily at his approach; and at night they followed him at a distance.

"What's the matter with me? Why do they treat me this way?" Juan Darién asked himself.

And not only did they flee from him, but also small boys shouted at him, "Get out of here. Go back where you came from! Go away!"

Grownups and elder people were no less hostile than the young boys. Who knows what would have happened if on the very afternoon of the festival the eagerly awaited animal tamer had not at last arrived. Juan Darién was in his house preparing the meager soup he had for supper when he heard the shouting of people rushing toward his house. Scarcely had he time to go out to see what it was before they seized him and dragged him to the animal tamer.

"Here he is!" they shouted, shaking him. "This is the one! He's a tiger! We don't want to know anything about tigers! Strip away his man-form and we'll kill him!"

And the boys, the fellow pupils whom he most loved, and even the old people, shouted, "He's a tiger! Juan Darién will devour us! Kill Juan Darién!"

Juan Darién—he was only a child of twelve—wept and protested as the blows rained down upon him. But at this moment the crowd parted and the animal tamer in his red jacket and his high patent leather boots, with his whip in his hand, appeared before Juan Darién. The tamer stared at him and firmly grasped the handle of his whip.

"Aha!" he exclaimed. "I recognized you all right! You can fool everyone except me! I see you, son of a tiger. Beneath your shirt I see the tiger stripes! Take off your shirt! Bring the hunting dogs! We'll soon see whether the dogs recognize you as a man or as a tiger!"

In a second they had torn off all Juan Darién's clothes and thrown him into a cage for wild beasts.

"Loose the dogs. Now!" the animal tamer said. "And commend yourself to your jungle gods, Juan Darién!"

And four ferocious dogs trained for hunting tigers were flung into the cage.

The animal tamer did this because dogs always recognize the scent of a tiger. He knew that their hunting dogs' eyes would see the tiger stripes hidden beneath the man-skin and, as soon as they smelled Juan Darién without his man's clothes, they would tear him to pieces.

But the only thing the dogs saw in Juan Darién was the good boy who loved even harmful animals. And they wagged their tails gently when they smelled him.

"Devour him! He's a tiger. Go! Go!" they shouted to the dogs. And the dogs barked madly and leaped around the cage, not knowing what to attack.

The test had not produced any results.

"Very well," the tamer exclaimed then. "These are bastard dogs, tiger-breed. They don't recognize him. But I recognize you, Juan Darién, and *now* we'll see."

And saying this, he entered the cage and raised his whip.

"Tiger!" he cried. "You're a tiger, but you're facing a man now. I can see your tiger stripes under that man-skin you've stolen! Show your stripes!"

And he struck Juan Darién's body with a ferocious blow from his whip. The poor naked creature howled with pain, while the crowd, inflamed, echoed, "Show your tiger stripes!"

The cruel torture proceeded for a while, but I don't want the children listening to me to see any being tortured this way.

"Please! I'm dying," shouted Juan Darién.

"Show your stripes," they replied.

"No, no! I'm a man! Ahh, Mama!" the unhappy child sobbed.

"Show your stripes," they replied.

Finally the torture ended. In a corner in the back of the cage, devastated, lay the little bleeding body of the child who had been

Juan Darién. He was still alive, and he could still walk when they pulled him out, but he was suffering more than anyone will ever know.

They pulled him from the cage, and, pushing him down the middle of the street, they drove him from the town. He was falling at every step, and behind him, pushing him, came children, women, and grown-up men.

"Get out of here, Juan Darién! Go back to the jungle, son of a tiger. Heart of a tiger. Get out, Juan Darién!"

And those who were at a distance and could not strike him threw rocks at him.

Juan Darién collapsed, finally, his poor child's hands outstretched in appeal. And cruel destiny had it that a woman standing in the doorway of her home and holding an innocent babe in her arms misunderstood his gesture of supplication.

"He tried to steal my baby!" the woman cried. "He stretched out his hands to kill him! He's a tiger! Let's kill him now, before he kills our children!"

Thus spoke the woman. And in this way the serpent's prophecy was fulfilled: Juan Darién would die when a mother among men exacted the life and the man's heart that another mother had given him at her breast.

No further accusation was necessary; the infuriated crowd was decided. Twenty hands holding stones were raised to crush Juan Darién when, from the rear, the tamer's hoarse voice ordered, "Let's brand him with stripes of fire! Let's burn him along with the fireworks."

It was already late, and by the time they arrived at the plaza the darkness had settled. In the plaza they had erected a huge fireworks display with wheels and crowns and Bengal lights. They tied Juan Darién to the top and set a match to one edge. A fiery thread raced up and down, lighting the entire display. And on high, amidst the fixed stars and the gigantic many-colored wheels, one could see the sacrifice of Juan Darién.

"This is your last day as a man, Juan Darién!" they all clamored. "Show your stripes!"

"Forgive me, forgive me!" the creature cried, writhing among the sparks and the clouds of smoke. The yellow, red, and green wheels whirled dizzily, some to the right and some to the left. Jets of flames at the edges of the display outlined its great circumference, and Juan Darién writhed in the center, burned by the streams of sparks shooting across his body.

"Show your stripes," they continued to roar below.

"No! Forgive me! I am a man!" the miserable creature still had time to cry out. After a new wave of fire one could see that his body was shaking convulsively; his moans were taking on a deeper, harsher timbre, and little by little his body was changing form.

With a savage yell of triumph the crowd finally could see the parallel, black, and fatal stripes of the tiger appearing beneath the human skin.

The atrocious act of cruelty was finished; they had achieved what they desired. On high, instead of a creature innocent of all blame, there was only the body of a tiger roaring in his death agony.

The Bengal lights were also fading. One last shower of sparks from a dying wheel reached the rope which bound the wrists (no: the paws of the tiger, for Juan Darién was no more), and the body fell heavily to the ground. The crowd dragged it to the edge of the jungle, abandoning it there for the jackals to devour the body and its beast's heart.

But the tiger had not died. With the cool of the night it revived, and in the grip of horrible torment it dragged itself deep into the jungle. For a whole month it kept to its refuge in the darkest part of the jungle, waiting with a beast's somber patience for its wounds to heal. Finally they all closed except one that would not heal, a deep burn in its side that the tiger covered with large leaves.

For from his previous existence the tiger had retained three things: a vivid memory of the past, the ability to use its hands (which it used like a man), and a language. But in every other way, it was absolutely and totally a beast, completely indistinguishable from other tigers.

When at last it felt cured, it spread the word to the other tigers in the jungle to meet that very night at the edge of the great canebrake that bordered the cultivated lands of the villagers. As night fell it set out silently for the village. On the outskirts the tiger climbed a tree and for a long time waited motionless. It saw pass beneath him, without even bothering to look, pitiful women and exhausted laborers of miserable aspect, until finally it saw a man in high boots and a red jacket coming down the road.

As the tiger gathered itself to spring, not a single branch moved. It leaped upon the animal tamer; with one slap of its paw it knocked the man unconscious; grasping his belt in its teeth, the tiger carried him unharmed to the great canebrake.

There, among canes so tall they obscured the ground from which they rose, the jungle tigers were pacing in the dark, their eyes like brilliant moving lights. The man was still unconscious. The tiger said, "Brothers, for twelve years I lived among men, like a man. And I am a tiger. Perhaps what I am about to do will erase that stain. Brothers, tonight I break the last tie that binds me to the past."

After saying this, the tiger grasped the still-unconscious man in its mouth and climbed to the highest point in the canebrake, where it left him tied between two bamboos. Then it set fire to some dry leaves on the ground, and soon a crackling blaze arose.

The frightened beasts retreated before the fire, but the tiger said to them, "Peace, brothers!" And they were calmed and, with their front paws crossed, stretched out on their bellies to watch.

The canebrake burned like an enormous fireworks display. The cane exploded like bombs, and the escaping gases crisscrossed like slim, brightly colored arrows. The flames ascended in swift muted puffs, leaving livid empty spaces; and at the summit, where the fire had not yet reached, the cane swayed, curling in the heat.

But the man, touched by the flames, had regained consciousness. He saw the tigers below with their reddish eyes raised toward him, and he understood.

"Forgive me, forgive me," he howled, twisting and turning. "I beg forgiveness for everything."

No one answered. The man then felt he had been abandoned by God, and he cried with all his soul, "Forgive me, Juan Darién!"

When he heard this, Juan Darién raised its head and coldly said, "There is no one here called Juan Darién. I do not know Juan Darién. That is a man's name, and here we are all tigers."

And turning toward its companions, as if it did not understand, it asked, "Is any one of you named Juan Darién?"

But now the flames were blazing high as the sky. And among the pointed Bengal lights shooting through the wall of flame could be seen a burning, smoking, black body.

"I'll soon be with you, brothers," said the tiger. "But there is still something I must do."

And once again it set out toward the village, followed, unnoticed, by the tigers. It stopped before a poor, sad garden, leaped over the wall, and, after passing by many stones and crosses, came to a halt before an unadorned piece of land where the woman it had called mother for eight years lay buried. The tiger knelt—it knelt like a man—and for a moment there was silence.

"Mother!" the tiger finally murmured with profound tenderness. "Only you among all humans recognized the sacred right to life that belongs to every being in the Universe. Only you recognized that man and tiger are different only in their hearts. You taught me to love, to understand, and to forgive. Mother! I am sure you hear me. I am your son forever, no matter what happens in the future, but *yours* only. Good-by, dear mother!"

And when the tiger rose, it saw the reddish eyes of its brothers observing it from behind the adobe wall, and once again it joined them.

At this moment from the depths of the night the warm wind carried to them the sound of a shot.

"It is from the jungle," the tiger said. "It is men. They are hunting and killing and slaughtering."

Turning then toward the village illuminated in the reflection of the burning jungle, it exclaimed, "Heartless and unredeemed race! Now it is *my* turn!"

And returning to the tomb where it had just prayed, the tiger tore the dressing from its wound with a sweep of its paw, and on the cross which bore its mother's name, with its own blood, wrote in large letters

AND
JUAN DARIÉN

"Now we are at peace," it said, and directing with its brothers a roar of defiance toward the terrified village, it concluded, "Now, to the jungle! And a tiger forever!"

With his machete the man had just finished clearing the fifth lane of the banana grove. Two lanes remained, but, since only chirca trees and jungle mallow were flourishing there, the task still before him was relatively minor. Consequently the man cast a satisfied glance at the brush he had cleared out and started to cross the wire fence so he could stretch out for a while in the grama grass.

But as he lowered the barbed wire to cross through, his foot slipped on a strip of bark hanging loose from the fence post, and in the same instant he dropped his machete. As he was falling, the man had a dim, distant impression that his machete was not lying flat on the ground.

Now he was stretched out on the grass, resting on his right side just the way he liked. His mouth, which had flown open, had closed again. He was as he had wanted to be, his knees doubled and his left hand over his breast. Except that behind his forearm, immediately below his belt, the handle and half the blade of his machete protruded from his shirt; the remainder was not visible.

The man tried to move his head— in vain. He peered out of the corner of his eye at the machete, still damp from the sweat of his hand. He had a mental picture of the extension and the trajectory of the machete in his belly, and coldly, mathematically, and inexorably he knew with certainty that he had reached the end of his existence.

Death. One often thinks in the course of his life that one day, after years, months, weeks, and days of preparation, he will arrive in his turn upon the threshold of death. It is mortal law, accepted and foreseen; so much so that we are in the habit of allowing ourselves to be agreeably transported by our imaginations to that moment, supreme among all moments, in which we breathe our last breath.

But between the present and that dying breath, what dreams, what reverses, what hopes and dramas we imagine for ourselves in our lives! A vigorous existence holds so much in store for us before our elimination from the human scene! Is this our consolation, the pleasure and the reason of our musings on death? Death is so distant, and so unpredictable is that life we still must live.

Still . . . ? Still not two seconds passed: the sun is at exactly the same altitude; the shadows have not advanced one millimeter. Abruptly, the long-term digressions have just been resolved for the man lying there; he is dying.

Dead. One might consider him dead in his comfortable position.

But the man opens his eyes and looks around. How much time has passed? What cataclysm has overtaken the world? What disturbance of nature does this horrible event connote?

He is going to die. Coldly, fatally, and unavoidably, he is going to die.

The man resists—such an unforeseen horror! And he thinks: it's a nightmare; that's what it is! What has changed? Nothing. And he looks: isn't that banana grove *his* banana grove? Doesn't he come every morning to clear it out? Who knows it as well as he? He sees the grove so perfectly, thinned out, the broad leaves bared to the sun. There are the leaves, so near, frayed by the wind. But now they are not moving. . . . It is the calm of midday; soon it will be twelve o'clock.

Through the banana trees, high up, the man on the hard ground sees the red roof of his house. To the left, a glimpse of the scrub trees and the wild cinnamon. That's all he can see, but he knows very well that behind his back is the road to the new port and that in the direction of his head, down below, the Paraná, wide as a lake, lies sleeping in the valley. Everything, everything, exactly as always: the burning sun, the vibrant air, the loneliness, the motionless banana trees, the wire fence with the tall, very thick posts that soon will have to be replaced. . . .

Dead! But is it possible? Isn't this one of many days on which he has left his house at dawn with his machete in his hand? And isn't his horse, his mare with the star on her forehead, right there just four meters away, gingerly nosing the barbed wire?

But yes! Someone is whistling. . . . He can't see because his back is to the road, but he feels the vibration of the horse's hooves on the little bridge. . . . It is the boy who goes by toward the new port every morning at 11:30. And always whistling. . . . From the bark-stripped post he can almost touch with his boot the live-thicket fence that separates the grove from the road; it is fifteen meters. He knows it perfectly well, because he himself had measured the distance when he put up the fence.

So what is happening, then? Is this or isn't it an ordinary midday like so many others in Misiones, in his bushland, on his pasture, in his cleared-out banana grove? No doubt! Short grass, and hills, silence, leaden sun . . .

Nothing, nothing has changed. Only he is different. For two minutes now his person, his living personality, has had no connection with the cleared land he himself spaded up during five consecutive months, nor with the grove, work of his hands alone. Nor with his family. He has been uprooted, brusquely, naturally, because of a slippery piece of bark and a machete in the belly. Two minutes: he is dying.

The man, very weary, lying on his right side in the grama grass, still resists admitting a phenomenon of such transcendency in the face of the normal, and monotonous, aspect of the boy who has just crossed the bridge as he does every day.

But it isn't possible that he could have slipped! The handle of his machete (it's worn down now; soon it will have to be changed for another) was grasped just right between his left hand and the barbed wire. After ten years in the woods, he knows very well how you manage a bush machete. He is only very weary from the morning's work and is resting a little as usual.

The proof? But he himself planted this grama grass that is poking between his lips in squares of land a meter apart! And that is his banana grove and that his starred mare snorting cautiously by the barbed wire! The horse sees him perfectly; he knows she doesn't dare come around the corner of the fence since he himself is lying almost at the foot of the post. The man distinguishes her very well, and he sees the dark threads of sweat on her crupper and withers. The sun is as heavy as lead, and the calm is great; not a fringe of the banana trees is moving. Every day he has seen the same things.

. . . Very weary, but he's just resting. Several minutes must have passed now. . . . And at a quarter to twelve, from up there, from his house with the red roof, his wife and two children will set out for the grove to look for him for lunch. He always hears, before anything else, the voice of his smaller son who tries to break away from his mother's hand: "Pah-pah! Pah-pah!"

Isn't that it . . . ? Of course, he hears it now! It's time. That's just what he hears, the voice of his son. . . .

What a nightmare! But, of course, it's just one of many days, ordinary as any other! Excessive light, yellowish shadows, oven-still heat that raises sweat on the motionless horse next to the forbidden banana grove.

. . . Very, very tired, but that's all. How many times, at midday like this, on his way to the house, has he crossed this clearing that was a thicket when he came, and virgin bush before that? He was always tired, slowly returning home with his machete dangling from his left hand.

But still he can move away in his mind if he wants; he can, if he wants, abandon his body for an instant and look at the ordinary everyday landscape from the flood ditch he himself built—the stiff grama grass in the field of volcanic rock, the banana grove and its red sand, the wire fence fading out of sight in the distance as it slopes downward toward the road. And, farther still, the cleared land, the work of his own hands. And at the foot of a bark-stripped post, thrown on his right side, his legs drawn up, exactly like any other day, he can see himself, a sunny little heap on the grama grass—resting, because he is very tired.

But the horse, striped with sweat, cautiously motionless at a corner of the fence, also sees the man on the ground and doesn't dare enter the banana grove, as she would like to. With the voices nearby now—"Pah-pah!"—for a long, long while, the mare turns her motionless ears toward the heap on the ground and finally, quieted, decides to pass between the post and the fallen man—who has rested now.

Anaconda

It was ten o'clock at night and suffocatingly hot. Haze hung heavy over the jungle, and not a breath of air was stirring. The carbon black sky was split intermittently from horizon to horizon by silent lightning flashes, but the hissing rainstorm to the south was still far away.

Down a cow path through the middle of white esparto grass Lanceolada [she-of-the-lance-shaped-head] advanced with all the generic slowness of serpents. She was a beautiful *yarará*, a meter and a half long, the black angles of her body clearly delineated, scale by scale. She advanced, testing the security of the terrain with her tongue, which in the ophidians perfectly replaces the function of fingers.

She was hunting. When she reached a crossing in the paths she stopped, very carefully coiled upon herself, settled herself more comfortably, and, after lowering her head to the level of her coils, adjusted her lower mandible and waited, motionless.

Five hours passed, minute after slow minute. At the end of this time she lay as motionless as when she had begun her vigil. A bad night! Day began to break, and she was about to retire when she changed her mind. An enormous shadow was silhouetted against the purplish eastern sky.

"I should go by the House," the *yarará* said to herself. "I haven't heard any noise for days, but one needs to keep on the alert. . . ."

Prudently, she glided toward the dark shadow.

The house to which Lanceolada was referring was an old white-washed wooden building surrounded by a veranda. Two or three sheds were scattered around the grounds. The building had been uninhabited from Time Immemorial. Now unexpected and unusual sounds were heard: the ring of iron against iron, the neigh of a horse, a combination of sounds that betrayed the presence of Man a mile away. A bad state of affairs. . . .

But one must make sure, which Lanceolada did much sooner than she had wished.

Through an open door she heard an unmistakable sound. The viper raised her head, and, as she noted that a cold clearness on the horizon was heralding the dawn, she saw a slim shadow, tall and strong, moving toward her. She heard footsteps, too—the strong, sure, enormously distanced thuds that announce the enemy a mile away.

"Man!" Lanceolada hissed. And quick as lightning she coiled in readiness.

The shadow was upon her. One enormous foot fell alongside her, and the *yarará*, with all the violence of the attack upon which one gambles his life, struck and then recoiled to her former position.

The man stopped; he thought he had felt a blow on his boots. Without moving his feet he surveyed the weeds around him but could see nothing in the darkness, barely broken now by the vague light of dawn, so he continued on his way.

Now Lanceolada could see that the House was beginning to take on life, real and effective life . . . MAN. The *yarará* retreated to her nest, taking with her the conviction that this nocturnal incident had been only the prologue to a great drama soon to unfold.

I I

The following day, Lanceolada's first preoccupation was the danger that, with the arrival of Man, would filter down upon the whole Family. Man and Devastation have been synonymous from Time Immemorial throughout the entire Kingdom of the Animals. For the Vipers, the poisonous snakes, particularly, the disaster was personified in two horrors: the searching machete that cut into the very belly of the jungle and the fire that suddenly annihilated the woods and, with it, the hidden lairs.

110

So it was urgent to prevent that disaster. Lanceolada waited for the coming of the following night to set her campaign in motion. Without much effort she found two companions to spread the alarm. She, for her part, searched until twelve o'clock for the most propitious place to hold the gathering. So at two o'clock in the morning the Congress found itself, if not complete, at least with the majority of the species present to decide what should be done.

At the base of a rampart of natural stone five meters high and, of course, deep in the woods, was a cavern hidden by the ferns that almost obscured the entrance. For a very long time it had served as a shelter for Terrífica, a rattlesnake ancient among the ancients whose tail boasted thirty-two rattles. She was only 140 centimeters long, but, on the other hand, in girth she was almost as thick as a bottle. She was a magnificent specimen, marked transversely with yellow rhomboids, vigorous, tenacious, capable of facing her enemy for seven hours without moving, quick to set the fangs with the canals that are—and who should know if not those superior to her in size—the most admirably constructed of all the venomous snakes.

Consequently it was there, before imminent danger, presided over by the rattlesnake, that the Congress of Vipers met. Besides Lanceolada and Terrífica, the rest of the *yararás* of the district were there: little Coatiarita, the Benjamin of the Family, with the very visible reddish lines along her sides and her particularly sharp-pointed head. Also there, negligently stretched out as if there were all sorts of reasons besides having her white and brown stripes upon long salmon-colored bands admired, was slim Neuwied, the model of beauty who had kept for herself the name of the naturalist who had identified her species. Cruzada was there—*víbora de la cruz*, called Viper of the Cross in the south—the powerful and audacious rival of Neuwied's beauty. Atrocious Atroz was there; a sufficiently oracular name she had; and last, Urutú Dorado, the golden Dorado *yararacusú*, discreetly hiding in the depth of the cavern her 170 centimeters of black velvet obliquely striped by golden bands.

It should be noted that the species *yarará* of the formidable genre *Lachesis*, to which all the members of the assembly except Terrífica belong, has long been famous for the ancient rivalry among its numbers for beauty of design and color. There are, in fact, few beings as generously endowed as they.

According to the laws of the vipers, scarce species or those without real dominion in the territory cannot preside over the assemblies of the Empire. For this reason Urutú Dorado, a magnificently deadly animal, but one whose species is very rare, cannot pretend to this honor, so she gracefully yields to the rattlesnake Terrífica, weaker than she, but abounding in miraculous numbers.

The quorum of the Congress, then, was established, and Terrífica opened the session.

"Sisters!" she said. "We have all been informed by Lanceolada of the ominous presence of Man. I think I interpret the desire of all of us in trying to save our Empire from enemy invasion. Only one measure will suffice, since experience has taught us that giving up our land does not remedy anything. This measure, you well know, is war against Man, war without truce or quarter, starting from this very night, to which every species will bring its particular virtues. I am proud in this circumstance to abandon my human designation: I am no longer a rattlesnake; I shall be *yarará*, like all of you. The *yararás*, who carry death as their black standard. We *are* death, sisters! Meanwhile, let one of you present propose a battle plan."

Everyone knows, at least in the Empire of the Vipers, that, although Terrífica is famously equipped in her fangs, she has little enough in her head. She knows it, too, and although she is incapable of conceiving a plan, by dint of being the ancient queen she possesses sufficient tact to remain quiet about it.

Then Cruzada, stretching herself, said, "I agree with Terrífica, but it is my opinion that, as long as we have no plan, we cannot and should not do anything. What I regret is the absence in this Congress of our venomless cousins the Snakes."

There was a long silence. Evidently the Vipers did not find this proposal too flattering. But Cruzada smiled vaguely and continued, "I regret that what is so is so. . . . But let me simply remind you that if among all of us we tried to kill a snake we would not succeed. I have nothing more to say."

"If you mean because of their resistance to venom," Urutú Dorado objected lazily from the depths of the grotto, "I think I alone might disenchant them of that. . . ."

"It isn't a matter of venom," Cruzada replied disdainfully. "I could handle that, myself," she added, with a sideways glance at the *yararacusú*. "It's a matter of strength, of their dexterity and nerve, whatever you want to call it. Qualities of battle that no one would attempt to deny our cousins. I insist that in a campaign, such as the one we want to undertake, the Snakes would be very helpful to us—more than helpful, absolutely necessary."

But the proposition was still unpopular.

"Why Snakes?" Atroz exclaimed. "They're contemptible."

"They have fish eyes," the presumptuous Coatiarita added.

"They make me sick," Lanceolada protested disdainfully.

"Maybe it's something else they make you . . . ," Cruzada murmured, looking at her slyly.

"Me," Lanceolada hissed, lifting her head haughtily. "I warn you, you cut a sorry figure here defending those wriggling worms!"

"If only our cousins the Hunters could hear you," Cruzada murmured ironically.

When they heard the name *Hunters*, every member of the assembly became excited.

"There's no reason to call them Hunters!" they shouted. "They're just snakes, that's all."

"They call *themselves* the Hunters!" Cruzada replied wryly. "And we *are* in Congress."

From Time Immemorial, the particular rivalry between the two *yararás* Lanceolada, daughter of the extreme north, and Cruzada, whose habitat extends more toward the south, has been legend among the Vipers—a question of beauty, according to the Snakes.

"Come, come!" Terrífica intervened. "Let Cruzada explain

why she wants the assistance of the Snakes, seeing they do not represent Death as we do."

"For that very reason!" Cruzada replied, calm now. "It is indispensable that we know what Man is doing in the House; and for that, one must go there, to the House itself. Well, that's not any easy undertaking, because if our standard is that of Death, so is Man's—death more speedy than our own. Snakes have an enormous advantage over us in agility. Any one of us could go and look. But would she return? Nobody is better suited for this role than Ñacaniná. These explorations are a part of her daily habits. From the roof of the House she could see, hear, and return to inform us about everything before daylight."

The proposition was so reasonable that this time the entire assembly agreed, although still with a certain residue of unwillingness.

"Who will go to look for her?" several voices asked.

Cruzada unwound her tail from a tree trunk and slipped forward.

"I will go," she said. "And will return quickly."

"That's right," Lanceolada called after her. "Since you're her protector, you'll know just where to find her!"

Cruzada still had time to turn toward her and flash out her tongue—a challenge to be attended to later.

III

Cruzada found Ñacaniná climbing a tree.

"Oh, Ñacaniná!" she called with a light hiss.

Ñacaniná heard her name, but she prudently abstained from answering until she was called a second time.

"Ñacaniná," Cruzada repeated, raising her hiss a half tone.

"Who's calling?" the snake responded.

"It is I, Cruzada!"

"Ah, cousin. . . . What do you want, dear adorable cousin?"

"I'm not here to joke, Ñacaniná. . . . Do you know what's going on in the House?"

"Yes, Man has arrived. . . . What else?"

"And do you know that we're holding a Congress?"

"Oh, no, I didn't know that!" Ñacaniná replied, slithering head first down the tree, as sure as if she were moving on a horizontal plane. "In that case something serious must be happening. What is it?"

"For the moment, nothing, but we've called a Congress precisely to avoid that anything *does* happen. In short: several men are known to be in the House, and it's known they plan to remain indefinitely. That's Death for us."

"I thought you were Death for *them*. . . . You never seem to get tired of saying it!!!" the snake murmured ironically.

"Enough of that! We need your help, Ñacaniná."

"What for? None of this affects me."

"You never know. It's your bad fortune to resemble us, the Venomous Ones. By looking after our interests, you would be looking after your own."

"Yes, I understand," Ñacaniná replied after a moment during which she evaluated the number of unfavorable contingencies resulting from her resemblance to the Vipers.

"Well, can we count on you?"

"What do I have to do?"

"Very little. Go immediately to the House and situate yourself there so you can see and hear everything that's happening."

"No, that *isn't* much," Ñacaniná replied negligently, rubbing her head against the tree trunk. "But the fact is, I have a sure meal up there. A wild turkey hen took a notion to nest there a couple of days ago."

"Perhaps you'll find something to eat at the House," Cruzada consoled her smoothly. Her cousin looked at her suspiciously. "Well, come on, let's go. First let's go by the Congress."

"Oh, no!" Ñacaniná protested. "Not that. I'll do you the favor, and gladly. But I'll come to the Congress when I return . . . , if I return. But to see that Terrífica's noisy rattles, Lanceolada's rat eyes, and Coralina's stupid face before I go . . . ! Oh, no!"

"Coralina isn't there."

"That doesn't matter. There's enough with the rest of you."

115

"All right, all right," Cruzada didn't want to press her advantage. "But if you don't slow down a little I won't be able to keep up with you."

In fact, even at top speed the *yarará* was unable to keep pace with—for her—the relatively slow slithering of the Ñacaniná.

"You wait, you're near the others," the snake said. And she darted off at full speed, leaving her venomous cousin behind in a flash.

I V

Fifteen minutes later the Hunter reached her destination. The lights were still on in the House. Through the wide open doors poured streams of light, and even from a distance Ñacaniná could see four men seated around a table.

If she could only avoid contact with a dog, she could reach her goal safely. Would they have dogs? Ñacaniná feared so. As a result she crept forward with great caution, especially as she approached the veranda.

Once on it, she looked around attentively. No dog in front of her, or to the right or the left. Yes, over there, through the men's legs she could see a black dog sleeping on his side.

The field, then, was free. She could hear from where she was but not see. She glanced overhead and in a moment had what she desired. She crawled up a ladder leaning against the wall and in a second settled herself in the free space between the wall and the roof and lay stretched across a beam. But, in spite of her precautions, she had dislodged an old nail which fell to the floor, and a man looked up toward the ceiling.

"It's all over!" Ñacaniná thought, holding her breath.

A second man also looked up. "What is it?" he asked.

"Nothing. I thought I saw something black up there."

"A rat."

"Ah, Man makes mistakes," the snake murmured to herself. "Or maybe a *ñacaniná*."

"But that Man hit the mark!" she hissed, readying herself for battle.

But the men paid no further attention, and for half an hour Ñacaniná watched and heard everything.

V

The House, the reason for the Jungle's concern, had been converted into a scientific establishment of the greatest importance. The particular abundance of vipers in this corner of the territory had been known for some time, and the National Government had decided to create an Antivenom Institute where serum could be prepared against the venom of vipers. The availability of the vipers was basic to this plan since it is well known that the paucity of vipers from which to extract the venom is the principal impediment to a vast and safe preparation of serum.

The new establishment could be set into operation almost immediately since the men had brought with them two animals, a horse and a mule, already almost completely immunized. They had organized the laboratory and the serpentarium.

The men had brought with them a large number of venomous serpents—those that had served to immunize the animals. Even so, the number of serpents would have to be augmented to an astonishing degree, for if one considers that a horse in the last stages of immunization needs six grams of venom for every injection (a quantity sufficient to kill 250 nonimmunized horses) he will understand that the number of available vipers such an Institute requires is very great indeed.

The work, particularly difficult at first, of organizing an installation in the jungle kept the Institute personnel up half the night making the plans for the laboratory and the rest of the project.

A man wearing dark glasses who seemed to be the chief asked, "And how are the animals today?"

"Not very good," a second man replied. "If we don't get a good collection today . . ."

Ñacaniná, motionless on the overhead beam, eyes and ears alert, began to relax. "It seems to me," she said to herself, "that my venomous cousins are worried over nothing. There's nothing particular to fear from these men. . . ."

And stretching her head forward so that the point of her nose protruded beyond the beam, she observed even more carefully.

And one misfortune evokes another.

"We had a bad day today," a third added. "We broke five test tubes. . . ."

Ñacaniná felt more and more inclined to compassion. "Poor men," she murmured. "They broke five tubes. . . ."

And as she prepared to abandon her hiding place to explore that innocent house, she heard: "On the other hand, the vipers are magnificent. They seem to like it here."

"Yessss?" the snake shuddered, her tongue flickering. "What did that hairy one in the white suit say?"

The man continued, "This place seems ideal. . . . And we need them urgently for the animals and for ourselves."

"Fortunately we'll have fabulous viper hunting around here. There's no mistaking, this is viper country."

"Aha . . . , aha . . . , aha . . . ," Ñacaniná murmured, wrapping herself around the beam as tightly as possible. "Things begin to look a little different. I'd better stay a while longer with these good people. . . . One learns curious things."

She heard such curious things that when a half hour later she felt it was time to retire, her head was so filled with newly acquired wisdom that she made a false movement and a third of her body dropped from the beam to thump against the wood wall. Since she had fallen headfirst, in an instant her head was pointed directly toward the table, her tongue flashing.

The *ñacaniná*, which attains a length of three meters, is courageous, certainly the most courageous of our serpents. She resists a serious attack by man, who is infinitely larger than she, by standing her ground. As her own courage makes her believe she is feared, our snake was somewhat surprised to see that the men, realizing what they faced, began to laugh calmly.

118

"It's a *ñacaniná*. . . . Good, she'll keep the rats out of the house."

"Rats," she hissed. And as she held her belligerent stance, one man finally arose.

"No matter how useful she is, she's still a feisty little devil. . . . One of these nights I'll find her looking for rats under my bed." And picking up a nearby pole, he rushed at Ñacaniná. The pole whistled by the intruder's head and hit the wall with a terrible thwack.

Now there are attacks and attacks. Outside her native jungle, surrounded by four men, Ñacaniná was not pleased with the odds. She quickly retreated, concentrating all her energy on the faculty that along with courage constitutes her other principal attribute—her incredible speed.

Pursued by barking, even tracked for a long while by the dog— which threw still more light on the problem confronting them— the snake reached the cavern. She ignored Lanceolada and Atroz and coiled herself to rest, completely exhausted.

VI

"At last!" they all exclaimed, making a circle around the explorer. "We thought you'd decided to stay with your friends, the Men. . . ."

"Humph!" murmured Ñacaniná.

"What news do you bring us?" Terrífica asked.

"Must we await an attack, or do we pay no attention to the Men?"

"Perhaps that would be better," Ñacaniná replied. "And move to the other side of the river."

"What . . . ? What do you mean?" they exploded. "Are you mad?"

"Listen, first."

"Speak, then!"

And Ñacaniná told them everything she had seen and heard:

the installation of the Antivenom Institute, its plans, its goals, and the decision of the men to hunt every viper in the country.

"*Hunt* us!" exploded Urutú Dorado, Cruzada, and Lanceolada, their pride wounded to the quick. "Kill us, you mean!"

"No, just hunt you. Pen you up, feed you well, and every twenty days extract your venom. Can you imagine an easier life?"

The assembly was stupefied. Ñacaniná had explained very well the use to which the venom collection was to be put, but what she had not explained was how the serum was to be obtained.

"An antivenom serum! That would mean a sure cure, the immunization of Men and animals against our bite, our Family condemned to perish of hunger right in our own native Jungle."

"Exactly," Ñacaniná corroborated. "That's it exactly."

For Ñacaniná, the danger was not as great. What did it matter to her and her sisters the Hunters, who hunted without fangs, by the strength of their muscles, whether those animals were immunized or not? She saw only one dark fact and that, the excessive similarity of a snake to a viper, a condition propitious for fatal errors. This was the basis for her interest in abolishing the Institute.

"I offer myself to begin the campaign," said Cruzada.

"Do you have a plan?" Terrífica, always short on ideas, asked anxiously.

"No plan. I will simply go out tomorrow afternoon hoping to come across one of the Men."

"Be careful!" said Ñacaniná persuasively. "There are several empty cages. Oh, and I forgot," she added, turning to Cruzada. "A while ago, when I left there . . . there is a very hairy black dog. . . . And I think he can follow a serpent's trail. Be careful."

"We'll see about that! But I request that the full Congress be called for tomorrow night. If I'm not there, well . . . none the worse."

But the assembly was reacting to the new surprise.

"A dog that follows our trails? Are you sure?"

"Almost sure. Watch out for that dog because he can do us more harm than all the men put together!"

"I'll take care of him!" exclaimed Terrífica, happy (without the need for any mental effort) to put into play the glands that at the slightest nervous contraction squirt venom through the canal in her fangs.

But now each viper was prepared to spread the word in her own district, and Ñacaniná, the great climber, was given the special charge of carrying the news to the trees, favorite kingdom of the snakes.

At three o'clock in the morning, the assembly dissolved. The vipers, returning to their normal routines, spread out in different directions, each unaware of the other's presence, silent and dark, while in the depths of the cavern Terrífica lay coiled, motionless, her hard glassy eyes fixed in a dream of a thousand paralyzed dogs.

VII

It was one o'clock in the afternoon. Through the fiery countryside, in the shelter of the clumps of *espartillo*, Cruzada crawled toward the House. She had no plan, nor did she think one necessary, except to kill the first Man she encountered. She reached the veranda and coiled herself there, waiting. A half hour passed. The suffocating heat that had reigned for three days was beginning to weigh upon the eyes of the *yarará* when she felt a mute tremble emanating from the room. Standing at the open door, only thirty centimeters from the viper's head, was the dog, the hairy black dog, his eyes hazy with sleep.

"Damned beast!" Cruzada said to herself. "I would have preferred a Man."

At this moment the dog stood still and sniffed the air and turned his head. . . . Too late! He choked back a howl of surprise and furiously shook his bitten muzzle.

"And that's the end of him," Cruzada murmured, rearranging herself in her coils. But as the dog was about to throw himself upon the viper, he heard his master's steps and arched his back, barking at the *yarará*. The man with the dark glasses appeared before Cruzada.

"What's going on?" another asked from the other side of the veranda.

"An *alternatus*. A good specimen," the man replied. And before the viper could defend herself, she felt herself strangled in a kind of noose tied at the end of a pole.

The viper gnashed her fangs to see herself in this predicament; she threshed and lunged; she tried in vain to free herself and curl around the pole. Impossible; she needed a point of support for her tail, that famous point of support without which even a powerful boa finds itself reduced to the most shameful impotence. The man carried her, dangling, and she was thrown into the serpentarium.

This area for the serpents consisted of a piece of land enclosed by sheets of smooth zinc. It was furnished with a few cages containing some thirty or forty vipers. Cruzada fell to the ground, where for a moment she lay coiled and throbbing beneath the fiery sun.

The installation was obviously temporary; large, shallow, pitch-covered boxes served as pools for the vipers, and several small shelters and piled rocks offered protection to the guests in this improvised paradise.

In a few seconds the *yarará* was surrounded and scrutinized by five or six fellow prisoners who had come to identify her species.

Cruzada recognized all of them except an enormous viper bathing herself in a wire mesh-enclosed cage. Who was she? She was completely unfamiliar to the *yarará*. Curious, in her turn, she slowly approached the stranger.

She approached so close that the other serpent rose in challenge. Cruzada smothered a stupefied hiss as she coiled defensively. The great viper's neck had swollen monstrously, something Cruzada had never seen. She was really extraordinary looking.

"Who are you?" Cruzada murmured. "Are you one of us?"

She meant, are you venomous. The other viper, convinced there was no intent of attack in the *yarará*'s approach, flattened her great swollen hood.

"Yes. But not from here; from very far away . . . , from India."

"What is your name?"

"Hamadrías . . . or Royal hooded cobra."

"I am Cruzada."

"Yes, you didn't have to tell me that. I have seen many of your sisters. When did they catch you?"

"Just now. I couldn't kill."

"It would have been better for you had they killed you."

"But I killed the dog."

"What dog? The one here?"

"Yes."

The cobra burst out laughing at the same moment Cruzada received another shock: the fleecy dog she thought she'd killed was barking!

"Surprised, are you?" Hamadrías added. "The same thing has happened to many others."

"But I bit him on the head," Cruzada answered, more and more bewildered. "I spent every last drop of venom. It is the patrimony of the *yarará* to empty the contents of our venom sacs in one attack."

"It doesn't matter whether you emptied your sacs or not."

"He can't die?"

"Yes, but we can't kill him. He's immunized. But you don't know what that means."

"I know!" Cruzada countered quickly. "Ñacaniná told us."

Then the cobra regarded her attentively.

"You seem intelligent to me."

"At least as intelligent as you," Cruzada replied.

Again the neck of the Asiatic serpent abruptly swelled, and again the *yarará* coiled in defense.

Both vipers stared at each other, as the cobra's hood slowly deflated.

"Intelligent and courageous," murmured Hamadrías. "Yes, I can talk to you. Do you know the name of my species?"

"Hamadrías, I suppose."

"Or *Naja bungaró* . . . Royal hooded cobra. We are, in relation to the common hooded cobra of India, what you are compared to one of those *coatiaritas*. And do you know what we feed on?"

"No."

123

"On American vipers . . . , among other things," she concluded, her head swaying before Cruzada.

Cruzada rapidly calculated the length of the foreign ophiophagous serpent.

"Two and a half meters?" she asked.

"A little more than that, my tiny Cruzada," Hamadrías replied, following Cruzada's gaze.

"You're a good size. About the length of Anaconda, one of my cousins. Do you know what she feeds on?" and she, in turn, stared at Hamadrías. "On Asiatic vipers!"

"Well said!" Hamadrías replied, again swaying. And after cooling her head in the water, she added lazily, "A cousin of yours, you said?"

"Yes."

"Nonvenomous, then?"

"That's right. That's precisely why she has such a great weakness for venomous foreigners."

But the Asiatic serpent, absorbed in her thoughts, was no longer listening.

"Listen to me," she said suddenly. "I've had enough of men, dogs, animals, and all this hell of stupidity and cruelty. You must understand, imagine what it's been like. . . . I've been closed up here in a cage like a rat for a year and a half, mistreated, periodically tortured. And what's worse, scorned . . . , handled like an old rag by vile men. And I, who have the courage, the strength, and the venom necessary to kill every one of them, am condemned to sacrifice my venom to the preparation of their antivenom serum. Can you realize what this means to my pride?" she concluded, peering closely into the *yarará*'s eyes.

"Yes," she replied. "What must I do?"

"There's one way, only one way you can get the last drops of revenge. Come close. I don't want the others to hear. It hinges on the point of support we need to unleash our strength. Our salvation depends on that point of support. Only . . ."

"What?"

The Royal cobra again stared at Cruzada.

"Only, you may die . . ."

"Just me?"

"Oh no. . . . They, some of the Men, will also die."

"That's all I want! Continue."

"Come closer still. Closer!"

The dialogue continued a few moments in such low voices that the body of the *yarará* rubbed against the wire mesh of Hamadrías's cage, shedding some of her scales. Suddenly, the cobra rose, swayed, and struck Cruzada three times. The vipers, who had been following events from a distance, shouted, "Look at that! She's killed her! She's a traitor!"

Cruzada, bitten three times in the neck, dragged herself heavily across the grass. Suddenly she lay motionless, and it was there an Institute employee found her three hours later when he entered the serpentarium. The man looked at the *yarará*, nudged her with his foot, rolled her over like a length of rope, and stared at her white belly.

"She's dead . . . good and dead," he muttered. "But of what?" He squatted down to look at the viper. The examination did not take long. On the neck, at the very base of the head, he noticed the unequivocal marks of venomous fangs.

"Hum," he said to himself. "This must be the *hamadrías*'s work. There she lies, coiled and staring at me as if I were another *alternatus*. I've told the director a dozen times that the mesh of that cage is too big. And there's the proof. . . . Oh, well," he concluded, grasping Cruzada by the tail and pitching her over the zinc fence, "one less varmint to take care of!"

He went to see the director: "The *hamadrías* has bitten the *yarará* you brought in a while ago. We'll get very little venom from her."

"What a bore," the director replied. "And we need that venom today. We have only one more tube of serum. Did the *alternatus* die?"

"Yes, I threw her over the fence. You want me to bring the *hamadrías*?"

"Yes, there's nothing we can do. But bring her for the second collection, two or three hours from now."

VIII

. . . She felt battered, exhausted. Her mouth was filled with dirt and blood. Where was she?

The dense haze before her eyes began to evaporate, and Cruzada raised her head to identify her surroundings. She saw. . . . She recognized the zinc fence, and suddenly she remembered everything: the black dog, the loop, and the plan of battle devised by the enormous Asiatic serpent in which she, Cruzada, was gambling her life. She remembered everything now that the paralysis caused by the venom was beginning to leave her. With the return of her memory came the full awareness of what she must do. Would there still be time?

She tried to drag herself forward, but in vain; her body undulated, but she could not move. She lay still a moment, her uneasiness increasing.

"I'm only thirty meters away!" she murmured. "Two minutes, one minute of strength, and I'll be there in time!"

And after a new effort she succeeded in inching forward, desperately dragging herself toward the laboratory.

She crossed the patio and reached the door at the moment that the employee held the *hamadrías* suspended from his hands, while the man with the dark glasses was introducing a watch crystal into the serpent's mouth. As Cruzada was still at the threshold, his hand moved to press the poison sacs.

"I won't have time!" she said hopelessly. But dragging herself forward in one last supreme effort, she bared her shining white fangs. The employee, feeling his bare foot burning from the bite of the *yarará*, yelled and jumped—not far, but enough so the dangling body of the Royal cobra twisted, and she swung her body toward the table where swiftly she coiled around the table leg. With this point of support, she jerked her head from the employee's hands and sank her fangs up to the gums into the left wrist of the man with the dark glasses—right in a vein.

That was it! Amidst the shouts, the Asiatic cobra and the *yarará* fled without pursuit.

"A point of support," the cobra hissed as she fled across the fields. "That's all I needed. Success at last!"

"Yes," the *yarará*, still in great pain, raced beside her. "But I hope we never have to do that again."

At the laboratory, two black strings of sticky blood dripped from the man's wrist. The venomous injection of a *hamadrías* in a vein is too serious for a mortal to sustain for very long—and the wounded man's eyes closed forever after four minutes.

IX

The Congress was complete. In addition to Terrífica and Ñacaniná and the *yararás*—Urutú Dorado, Coatiarita, Neuwied, Atroz, and Lanceolada—Coralina had also arrived, a viper who, according to Ñacaniná, is a bit stupid, a fact that does not prevent her bite from being one of the most painful in the Kingdom. Besides, she is beautiful, uncontestably beautiful with her red and black rings.

As vipers are known to be very vain on the question of beauty, Coralina was quite happy about the absence of her sister Frontal, whose triple black and white rings upon a purple background place this coral viper on the highest scale of ophidic beauty.

The Hunters were represented that night by Drimobia, whose fate it is to be called the bush *yararacusú*, although her appearance is really quite different from theirs. Cipó also attended, a beautiful green, and a great hunter of birds. Radinea was there, small and dark, who ordinarily never abandons her puddles. Also Boipeva, whose primary characteristic is to flatten herself against the ground the moment she feels menaced. And Trigemine, a coral snake with a very delicate body like that of her tree-dwelling companions. And finally Esculapia, whose entrance, for reasons that will be clear in a moment, was greeted by generally uneasy glances.

Thus several species of both the venomous serpents and the Hunters were missing, an absence which requires an explana-

tion. When we said the Congress was complete, we were referring to the great majority of the species and especially those that
can be called *royal* because of their importance. From the first
Congress of Vipers it is remembered that the species with great
numbers, comprising the majority, could support their decisions
by strength of numbers. This was the reason for the numbers
present, even though the absence of the *yarará* Surucucú, whom
no one had been able to find, was deeply regretted. All the more
so because this viper, which reaches three meters in length, is,
besides being queen of America, also vice-empress of the World
Empire of Vipers, since only one snake surpasses her in size and
in potency of venom: the Asiatic *hamadrías*.

Someone else was missing, besides Cruzada, but all the Vipers
pretended not to notice her absence. Nevertheless, they were
forced to turn around when they heard a sound and turned to see
a head with large burning eyes peering through the ferns.

"May I enter?" the visitor said happily.

As if an electric current had passed through their bodies, the
Vipers raised their heads in unison when they heard that voice.

"What do you want here?" Lanceolada cried with profound
irritation.

"You have no place here!" Urutú Dorado exclaimed, for the
first time showing signs of vivacity.

"Get out! Get out!" cried several Vipers, intensely uneasy.

But Terrífica, with a clear, although tremulous, hiss, succeeded in making herself heard.

"Sisters. Don't forget we are in Congress, and all of us here
know its laws: nobody, while it is in session, may exercise any act
of violence. Enter, Anaconda!"

"Well said!" exclaimed Ñacaniná ironically. "The noble words
of our queen assure us. Enter, Anaconda!"

And the lively and pleasant head of Anaconda advanced, followed by all two and a half meters of dark sinuous body. She
passed all of them, exchanging an intelligent glance with Ñacaniná, and coiled herself, with light hisses of satisfaction, beside
Terrífica, who could not help but shudder.

"Do I disturb you?" Anaconda asked courteously.

"No, not at all!" Terrífica replied. "It's my venom sacs that make me uncomfortable, so swollen. . . ."

Anaconda and Ñacaniná again exchanged an ironic glance and then attended to the proceedings.

The very obvious hostility of the assembly toward the new arrival had a sound basis which one cannot help but appreciate. The anaconda is the queen of all snakes there are or ever will be, with the exception of the Malayan python. Her strength is phenomenal, and there is no animal of flesh and bone capable of resisting her embrace. When her ten meters of smooth black-spotted body begins to slip from the foliage of the tree, the entire jungle shivers and quakes. But Anaconda is too powerful to hate anyone—with one exception—and the knowledge of her own courage allows her to maintain a good friendship with man. If she detests anyone, it is, naturally, the venomous serpents—thus the commotion of the vipers.

Anaconda is not, however, a daughter of the region. Swimming in the foamy waters of the Paraná, she had arrived in this area during a great flood and continued to remain in the region, quite content with the country, enjoying good relations with everyone, in particular with Ñacaniná, with whom she'd formed a warm friendship. She was, furthermore, a young anaconda who still had a long way to go before reaching the ten meters of her happy grandparents. But the two and a half meters she already measured were equal to twice that length if one considers the strength of this magnificent boa, who for entertainment at dusk swam the Amazon with half her body raised out of the water.

But Atroz had just taken the floor before the now distracted Assembly.

"I think we should begin now," she said. "First of all, we must find out what happened to Cruzada. She promised to return immediately."

"What she promised," Ñacaniná intervened, "was to be here as soon as she could. We must wait for her."

"Why?" replied Lanceolada, not deigning to turn her head toward the snake.

"What do you mean, why?" Ñacaniná exclaimed, raising her

head. "Only a stupid *lanceolada* would say a thing like that . . . ! I'm already tired of hearing stupid remark after stupid remark in this Congress. You'd think the Venomous Vipers represented the entire Family. Everyone, except this one," she pointed with her tail toward Lanceolada, "knows that our plan depends on the news Cruzada brings us. Why wait for her? We are in bad shape if minds capable of asking such a question dominate in this Congress!"

"Don't be insulting," Coatiarita reproached her gravely.

Ñacaniná turned toward her. "And why are you getting into this?"

"Don't be insulting," the tiny viper repeated with dignity.

Ñacaniná contemplatively considered the punctilious Benjamin, and her voice changed.

"Tiny little cousin is right," she concluded tranquilly. "Lanceolada, I beg your forgiveness."

"It isn't important," the *yarará* replied with rage.

"It *isn't* important; but again, I ask you to forgive me."

Fortunately, Coralina, who was watching the entrance to the cavern, entered and hissed, "Here comes Cruzada!"

"At last!" exclaimed the assembled serpents happily. But their joy was transformed into stupefaction when, following the *yarará*, there entered an enormous viper totally unknown to them.

As Cruzada crossed to lie beside Atroz, the intruder slowly and gently coiled herself in the center of the cavern, then lay motionless.

"Terrífica!" said Cruzada. "Welcome our guest. She is one of us."

"We are sisters!" the rattlesnake hastened to say, observing her uneasily.

All the vipers, dying with curiosity, slithered toward the new arrival.

"She looks like a nonvenomous cousin," said one, a little disdainfully.

"Yes," another agreed. "She has round eyes."

"And a long tail."

"And besides . . ."

Suddenly they were struck dumb as the stranger's neck swelled monstrously. This lasted only a second; the hood deflated as the new arrival turned to her friend, her voice altered.

"Cruzada, tell them not to come so close. . . . I can't control myself."

"Yes, leave her alone!" Cruzada exclaimed. "Especially," she added, "since she has just saved my life . . . perhaps all our lives."

That was all that was necessary. For a while the Congress hung on Cruzada's every word; she had to tell it all: the encounter with the dog, the noose of the man in the dark glasses, the *hamadrías*'s magnificent plan, the final catastrophe, and the deep dream that had overcome the *yarará* until just an hour ago.

"The result," she concluded: "two men out of combat, and two of the most dangerous. Now all we have to do is to eliminate the others."

"Or the horses!" said Hamadrías.

"Or the dog!" added Ñacaniná.

The Royal cobra insisted, "The horses, I believe. I offer this as a basic fact: as long as the horses live, one man alone can prepare thousands of tubes of serum, with which they will immunize themselves against us. Rarely—you well know—does the occasion present itself to strike a vein, as it did yesterday. So I insist we must direct our attack against the horses. Then we shall see! As far as the dog is concerned," she concluded, glancing out of the corner of her eye at Ñacaniná, "he's beneath contempt."

It was evident that from the first moment the Asiatic serpent and the indigenous Ñacaniná had taken a dislike to one another. If one, in her role as a venomous reptile, represented an inferior type to the Hunter, the latter, because she was strong and agile, provoked the hatred and jealousy of Hamadrías. So the old and tenacious rivalry between venomous and nonvenomous serpents seemed about to become even more strong in this final Congress.

"In my opinion," answered Ñacaniná, "I believe that the

horses and Men are secondary in this struggle. No matter what good fortune we might have in eliminating them, that is nothing compared to the fortune the dog will enjoy the first day it occurs to them to beat the bush, and they will do it, be assured, before twenty-four hours pass. A dog immunized against any bite, even that of this lady with the sombrero in her throat," she added, pointing sideways at the Royal cobra, "is the most fearful enemy we can have, especially if one remembers that this enemy has been trained to follow our trail. What do you think, Cruzada?"

Everyone in the Congress was aware of the singular friendship that united the viper and the snake; possibly, more than friendship, it was a reciprocal awareness of their mutual intelligence.

"I agree with Ñacaniná," she replied. "If the dog is set on us, we are lost."

"But we will strike first," said Hamadrías.

"There's no way we can strike first! I am definitely for the cousin's plan."

"I was sure you would be," said the snake calmly.

This was more than the Royal cobra could hear without her rage rising to fill her fangs with venom.

"I don't know to what point we should value the opinion of this talky little señorita," she said, turning her slanted glance toward Ñacaniná. "The real danger in this affair is for us, the Venomous ones who have Death as our black standard. The Snakes know very well that Man doesn't fear them, since they're completely incapable of doing him any harm."

"Now that's really well said!" said a voice unheard before.

Hamadrías, who thought she had noticed a vague irony in the tranquil tone of that voice, whirled and saw two great brilliant eyes observing her placidly.

"Are you speaking to me?" she asked disdainfully.

"Yes, to you," the interrupter replied calmly. "Your statement is fraught with profound truth."

The Royal cobra again sensed the same irony, and, as if by presentiment, she measured with a glance the length of the interlocutor's body, coiled in the shadow.

"You are Anaconda!"

"That is correct," Anaconda replied, bowing her head. But Ñacaniná wanted to clarify everything once and for all.

"One moment!" she exclaimed.

"No," interrupted Anaconda. "Allow me, Ñacaniná. When one is well formed, agile, strong, and swift, he overpowers his enemy with the energy of nerves and muscles that constitute his honor—as do all the fighters of creation. Thus does the hawk hunt, the jaguar, the tiger; so do we hunt, all beings of noble build. But when one is dull, heavy, not too intelligent, and incapable, therefore, of fighting openly for life, then one is given a pair of fangs to assassinate by treachery . . . , like that imported lady who hopes to dazzle us with her great sombrero."

And in fact the Royal cobra, beside herself with rage, had dilated her monstrous neck, preparing to throw herself upon the insolent speaker. But, upon seeing this, the entire Congress rose menacingly.

"Be careful!" several shouted. "Our Congress is inviolable!"

"Lower your hood," Atroz rose, her eyes like burning coals.

Hamadrías turned toward her with a hiss of rage.

"Lower your hood," Urutú Dorado and Lanceolada slid forward.

Hamadrías had an instant of mad rebellion, thinking of the facility with which she could have destroyed one after another of her rivals. But seeing the belligerent attitude of the entire Congress, she slowly lowered her hood.

"Very well," she hissed. "I respect the Congress. But I ask that once we have adjourned . . . don't provoke me!"

"No one will provoke you," said Anaconda.

The cobra turned toward her with concentrated loathing. "Especially not *you*, because you fear me!"

"*I* fear you?" said Anaconda, advancing toward her.

"Peace, peace!" everyone shouted. "We are setting a very bad example. Let us decide what we must do!"

"Yes, it is time for that," said Terrífica. "We have two plans before us: Ñacaniná's proposal and that of our ally. Do we begin by attacking the dog, or do we throw all our forces against the horses?"

Well, although the majority was perhaps inclined to adopt the snake's plan, the bearing, size, and intelligence demonstrated by the Asiatic serpent had favorably impressed the Congress in her favor. Her magnificent attack against the personnel of the Institute was still vivid in their minds; and whatever might become of her new plan, it was certain that they already owed her for the elimination of two men. Add to that the fact that, except for Ñacaniná and Cruzada, who had already been in the campaign, none realized the terrible enemy an immunized, snake-tracking dog could be. Then you will understand why the Royal cobra's plan finally triumphed.

Although it was already very late, since it was a question of life or death, they decided to set out immediately.

"Forward, then," concluded the rattlesnake. "Does anyone have anything more to say?"

"Nothing!" shouted Ñacaniná. "Except that we'll be sorry!"

And the vipers and the snakes, all the species, prepared to advance toward the Institute.

"One last word!" warned Terrífica. "As long as the campaign lasts, we are still in Congress and we are not free to harm one another. Is that understood?"

"Yes, yes, enough words!" they all hissed.

The Royal cobra, as Anaconda was passing, looked at her somberly and said, "Later . . ."

"Certainly," Anaconda dismissed her happily, speeding like an arrow to the vanguard.

X

The personnel of the Institute were keeping watch over the peon who had been bitten by the *yarará*. Soon it would be dawn. An employee looked out the window where warm night air was entering and thought he heard a noise in one of the sheds. He listened awhile and said, "I think it's in the horses' shed. Go see, Fragoso."

So Fragoso lighted a lantern and went outside while the others listened, attentive, alert.

No more than half a minute had passed when they heard hurried steps on the patio, and Fragoso appeared, pale with surprise.

"The stable is filled with snakes!" he cried.

"Filled?" the new chief asked. "What do you mean? What's going on?"

"I don't know. . . ."

"Let's go."

And they rushed outside.

"Daboy! Daboy!" the chief called to the dog, moaning in his dreams, lying beneath the sick man's bed. And they all ran to the stable.

There, in the light of the lantern, they could see the horses and the mule kicking and defending themselves against the seventy or eighty snakes inundating the stable. The animals were whinnying and kicking against the stall, but the snakes, as if directed by a superior intelligence, were avoiding their blows, striking with fury.

The men, impelled forward by their precipitous entrance, fell amidst them. At the sudden blaze of light, the invaders stopped for an instant only to throw themselves, hissing, into a new assault in which, given the confusion of men and horses, it was difficult to determine which was the target.

Thus the personnel of the Institute saw themselves completely surrounded by snakes. Fragoso felt the thud of fangs against his boot tops, only a half centimeter from his knee, and he struck at the attacker with his stick—the hard flexible stick always available in a house in the bush. The new director chopped another serpent in half, and the other employee crushed, on the very neck of the dog, the head of a large viper that had wound itself with alarming swiftness around the animal's body.

All this took less than ten seconds. The sticks rained furious blows upon the always-advancing vipers striking at their boots and attempting to climb their legs. Amidst the whinnying of the horses, the shouts of the men, the dog's barking, and the hissing of the snakes, the assaulting troops were gaining more and more advantage over the defenders when Fragoso, throwing himself at an enormous viper he thought he recognized, stepped on a body and fell: the lamp shattered into a thousand pieces and went out.

"Fall back," yelled the new director. "Here, Daboy!"

And they rushed back to the patio, followed by the dog, who fortunately had been able to disentangle himself from the skein of vipers.

Pale and panting, they looked at one another.

"That was the work of the devil," the chief murmured. "I've never seen anything like it. What's the matter with the snakes of this region? Yesterday, two men bitten, as if mathematically planned. . . . Today . . . Luckily, they are unaware that they saved the horses for us with their bites. It will soon be dawn, and then it will be different."

"I thought I saw the Royal cobra among them," Fragoso ventured as he bandaged his aching wrist muscles.

"Yes," the other employee added. "I saw her clearly. And Daboy, is he all right?"

"Yes, he's terribly bitten. . . . Fortunately he can resist anything they give him."

The men again returned to the sick man whose respiration had now improved. He was drenched in sweat.

"It's beginning to get light," the new director said, looking out the window. "You stay here, Antonio. Fragoso and I are going out."

"Shall we take the nooses?" asked Fragoso.

"Oh, no," the chief replied, shaking his head. "We could have caught any other vipers in a second. But these are different. We'll take sticks and, certainly, the machete."

XI

The enemy that had assaulted the Antivenom Institute was not any different but simply vipers who had, before an enormous danger, countered with the collective intelligence of the species.

The sudden darkness following the broken lantern had warned the combatants of the danger of more light and more resistance. Furthermore, they could feel in the humidity the imminence of day.

"If we wait a moment longer," Cruzada exclaimed, "they'll cut off our retreat. Fall back!"

"Fall back, fall back," they all shouted. And slithering and sliding over one another, they rushed toward the fields. They moved as in a troop, frightened, routed, seeing with consternation that day was beginning to break in the distance.

They had been fleeing for twenty minutes when a sharp, clear bark, still distant, stopped the panting column.

"One minute," shouted Urutú Dorado. "Let's see how many we are and what we can do."

In the faltering light of dawn they examined their forces. Eighteen serpents had died under the hooves of the horses, among them two coral snakes. Atroz had been chopped in two by Fragoso, and Drimobia lay behind, her skull crushed as she strangled the dog. Coatiarita, Radinea, and Boipeva were also missing—in all, twenty-three combatants annihilated. Those remaining, without exception, were bruised, stepped on, kicked, their broken scales covered with dust and blood.

"A fine testimony to the success of our campaign," Ñacaniná said bitterly, stopping for an instant to rub her head against a stone. "Congratulations, Hamadrías!"

But she kept to herself what she had heard—since she had been the last to leave—from behind the closed door of the stable. Instead of killing, they had saved the horses who had been dying precisely because they needed venom! (It is known that for a horse that is being immunized, venom is as indispensable for its daily life as water itself, and it dies if it fails to receive it.)

A second barking sounded behind them on their trail.

"We are in imminent danger!" Terrífica shouted. "What shall we do?"

"To the grotto!" some shouted, slithering forward at full speed.

"They're mad!" Ñacaniná cried, as she ran. "They will all be crushed there. They're going to their death! Listen to me: we must scatter!"

The fugitives paused, irresolute. In spite of their panic, something told them that disbanding *was* the only means of salvation, and, madly, they looked in all directions. One single voice in support, one single voice, and it would be decided.

But the Royal cobra, humiliated, defeated in her second attempt at domination and filled with hatred for a country that from this time forward would be eminently hostile, preferred to lose everything, dragging down all the other species with her.

"Ñacaniná is mad," she exclaimed. "We must not separate. . . . It will be different there. To the cavern!"

"Yes, to the cavern," responded the terrified column of serpents, fleeing. "To the cavern!"

Ñacaniná saw that all clearly, understood that they were going to their deaths. Abject, routed, maddened with panic, the vipers were going to sacrifice themselves in spite of everything. And with a haughty flicker of her tongue, she, who could easily have saved herself with her speed, moved with the others directly toward death.

She felt a body by her side and was happy to recognize Anaconda.

"You see now," Ñacaniná said to her with a smile, "what the Asiatic serpent has brought us to."

"Yes, she's an evil one," murmured Anaconda, as she raced along beside her.

"And now she's leading all the others to a massacre!"

"At least," Anaconda noted with a somber voice, "she will not live to have that pleasure."

And with a burst of speed, the two caught up with the column.

They had arrived.

"One moment!" Anaconda moved forward, her eyes shining. "You do not know it, but I know with certainty that within ten minutes there will not be a one of us alive. The Congress, and its laws, therefore, are concluded. Is that not so, Terrífica?"

There was a long silence.

"Yes," Terrífica murmured wearily. "It is concluded."

"Then," continued Anaconda, turning her head in all directions, "before I die, I would like . . . Ah, that's better!" she stopped, satisfied, as she saw the Royal cobra advancing slowly toward her.

That was probably not the ideal moment for a combat. But since the world is the world, nothing, not even the presence of Man hovering over them, can prevent a Viper and a Hunter from solving their private affairs.

The first blow favored the Royal cobra: her fangs sank to the gums in Anaconda's neck. Anaconda, with the boa's marvelous maneuver of turning an almost mortal blow into an attack, lashed her body forward like a whip and wrapped it around Hamadrías, who felt its strangling force in an instant. The boa, concentrating her life in that embrace, progressively closed her rings of steel, but the Royal cobra did not loosen her hold. There was even an instant when Anaconda felt her head crack between Hamadrías's teeth. But she succeeded in one last supreme effort, and this last flash of will tipped the balance in her favor. Dripping slather, the mouth of the semiasphyxiated cobra loosened its hold, while the anaconda, her head freed, in turn pressed the attack on the *hamadrías's* body.

Sure of the terrible embrace with which she immobilizes her rival, Anaconda inched her mouth with its short, rough teeth little by little up her rival's neck as the cobra desperately flailed in the paralyzing grip. The ninety-six sharp teeth of the anaconda climbed, reached the throat, and climbed still, until, with a muffled, prolonged crunch of cracked bones, she clamped her mouth around her enemy's head.

It was all over. The boa loosened her coils, and the battered body of the dead Royal cobra slithered heavily to the ground.

"At least I am happy," Anaconda murmured, falling lifeless upon the dead body of the Asiatic serpent.

It was in that instant that the vipers heard less than a hundred meters away the sharp barking of the dog.

And they, who less than ten minutes before had trampled, terrified, over one another to the entrance of the cavern, now felt flame rise to their eyes, the savage call of the battle to the death.

"Let's go inside!" some called, nevertheless.

"No! Here! We die here!" They choked in smothered hisses. And before the stone wall that cut off any possibility of retreat, necks and heads raised on coiled bodies, eyes like coals, they waited.

They did not have long to wait. Against the black bush in the still unclear light of day emerged the two tall silhouettes of the new director and Fragoso, holding a dog mad with rage straining forward on his leash.

"It's all over. Definitely this time," murmured Ñacaniná, with these six words bidding farewell to the happy life she had decided to sacrifice. And with a violent push she threw herself against the unleashed dog who fell upon the serpents, his mouth foaming. The animal dodged her attack to fall furiously upon Terrífica, who buried her fangs in the dog's muzzle. Daboy shook his head frantically, thrashing the rattlesnake in the air, but she would not release her hold.

Neuwied took advantage of the instant to sink her fangs into the animal's belly, but also at this moment the men joined in the attack. In a second Terrífica and Neuwied were dead, crushed. Urutú Dorado was chopped in half, and also Cipó. Lanceolada managed to catch hold of the dog's tongue, but two seconds later she fell beside Esculapia, chopped in three pieces by the double attack.

The combat—rather, the extermination—continued furiously amidst hisses and the hoarse barking of Daboy, who seemed to be everywhere at once. One after another they fell without mercy—

but they had not sought mercy—their heads crunched between the dog's jaws or crushed by the men. They were massacred before the cavern where they had held their last Congress. And among the last to fall were Cruzada and Ñacaniná.

Not one was left. Triumphant for the day, the men sat down and contemplated the total massacre of the species. Daboy, panting at their feet, showed some signs of poison in spite of being powerfully immunized. He had been bitten sixty-four times.

As the men rose to leave, for the first time they noticed Anaconda, who was beginning to revive.

"What is this boa doing here?" the new director asked. "This isn't her territory. From the looks of it, she took on the Royal cobra, and in her way, avenged us. If we could save her, we'd be doing a great thing. She seems terribly poisoned. Let's take her along. Perhaps some day she'll save us from this whole lot of vipers."

So they left. On a pole between their shoulders they carried a wounded and exhausted Anaconda, who was thinking of Ñacaniná, whose destiny, with a little less arrogance, could have been similar to hers.

Anaconda did not die. She lived a year with the men, inquisitive, observing everything about her, until one night she escaped. But the story of the long months of this voyage up the Paraná, beyond Guayrá, still further to the lethal gulf where the Paraná assumes the name of the river Death, the strange life that Anaconda lived, and the second voyage she undertook with her brothers upon the dirty waters of a great flood—this story of rebellion and the assault of the water plants belongs to another story.

The Incense
Tree Roof

In the state of Misiones, around and amidst the ruins of San Ignacio, the second capital of the Jesuitical empire, rises the present town of the same name—San Ignacio. It is composed of a number of small properties hidden from each other by trees. At the edge of the ruins, on a bare hill, rise a few rude houses bleached blinding white by the sun and lime but graced at sunset with a magnificent view of the valley of the Yabebirí river. There are stores in the district, more than the heart could desire, to the point that it is impossible for a new road to open up without a German, a Spaniard, or a Syrian setting up shop on the spot. All the public offices are located within the space of two blocks: the police station, the justice of the peace, the city offices, and a coeducational school. As a note of local color, there is a bar constructed on these same ruins—overrun, as you know, by vegetation—a bar created in the days of the fever for yerba maté, the tea that became the national drink of the area, when the plantation foremen coming down the Upper Paraná toward Posadas eagerly debarked in San Ignacio to sit, blinking tenderly, before a bottle of whiskey. I have related the characteristics of that bar in another story so we won't go into that again today.

But in the time we're talking about, not all the public offices were actually located in the town. Between the ruins and the new port, a half-league from each, on a magnificent mesa chosen for the private delight of its inhabitant, lived Orgaz, the chief of the Bureau of Records, and this public office was located in his house.

Orgaz's house was made of wood, with a roof of incense tree shingles layered like slate. This is an excellent arrangement if you use dry shingles that have been drilled for nail holes ahead of time. But when Orgaz raised his roof, the wood was newly split, and he drove the nails right through the shakes, with the result that the wooden shingles split and curled up at the ends till the bungalow roof resembled a sea urchin. Every time it rained, Orgaz had to change the position of his bed eight or ten times, and all his furniture was marred with whitish water spots.

We have emphasized this detail of Orgaz's house because the sea-urchin roof was what absorbed the chief of the Bureau of Record's energies for four years, scarcely allowing him time, during brief periods of respite, to sweat through his siesta time stringing wire or to disappear into the bush, reappearing a couple of days later with leaves and twigs in his hair.

Orgaz was a great nature lover, who, during his bad moments, spoke very little and listened to others with an attentive but slightly insolent air. He was not liked in the town, but he was respected.

In spite of Orgaz's absolute sense of democracy and his feeling of brotherhood and even, at times, hilarity with the genteel men—all in correct breeches—of yerba and authority, there was always an icy barrier separating them. No one could say there was the least trace of haughtiness in any of Orgaz's actions. But it was precisely this—haughtiness—of which he was accused.

Certain incidents, however, had given rise to this impression.

In the first days of his arrival in San Ignacio, when Orgaz was not yet an official and was still living alone on his plateau constructing his spiny roof, he received an invitation from the director of the school to visit the establishment. The director, naturally, felt flattered to do the honors of his school for an individual of Orgaz's culture.

Orgaz set out the following morning wearing his usual blue pants, boots, and linen shirt. But his route took him through the bush, where he came upon an enormous lizard he wanted to catch alive. So in order to take it with him, he tied a string of liana around the lizard's belly. He emerged from the bush, finally, at the door of the school where the director and his teachers were awaiting him; but he made his grand entrance in torn shirt sleeves, dragging his lizard by the tail.

Also, during that time, Bouix's burros helped foment the opinion that was growing about Orgaz.

Bouix was a Frenchman, who had lived thirty years in this country and considered it his own. His animals ranged free, devastating his hapless neighbor's plantings. The dumbest calf in Bouix's herds was still smart enough to rub his head up and down for hours to loosen the strands of a wire fence. They didn't have barbed wire in those days. And when it was introduced, there were still Bouix's burros, who would throw themselves beneath the lowest strand and dance on their sides until they worked their way beneath the fence. But no one complained: Bouix was justice of the peace in San Ignacio.

When Orgaz arrived there, Bouix was no longer judge. But his burritos didn't know that, and every evening they would trot down the road looking for a tender planting; when they found one they would stand and examine it across the wire, their lips tremulous and their ears laid back against their heads.

When it came his turn to be devastated, Orgaz bore it patiently; he strung some wire, and occasionally would get up in the middle of the night to run naked through the dew, chasing the burritos who had come up as far as his tent. He went, finally, to complain to Bouix, who solicitously called all his sons together to request they take better care of the burritos who were bothering "poor señor Orgaz." The burritos continued to run loose, and Orgaz returned a couple of times to see the taciturn Frenchman, who once again commiserated and clapped his hands to summon his sons . . . with the same result as before.

Then Orgaz placed a sign on the main road that read:

Warning! The grass in this pasture is poisoned!

For ten days he had peace. But the following night he again heard the stealthy little steps of the burros ascending the hill, and a little later he heard the rac! rac! of leaves being torn from his palms. Orgaz lost his patience, and, again running out naked, he shot the first burro he saw.

The following morning he sent a boy to inform Bouix that at dawn he had found a dead burro at his place. Bouix himself did not go to verify this unlikely happening but sent his eldest son, a great brawny boy as tall as he was swarthy, and as swarthy as he was somber. This gloomy boy read the sign as he came through the gate, and in bad humor he strode up the hill to where Orgaz stood waiting for him with his hands thrust in his pockets. Scarcely bothering to greet him, Bouix's delegate approached the dead burro. Orgaz, in his turn, also moved closer. The boy circled the burro a couple of times, examining him from every angle.

"Yep. He died last night, all right," he muttered finally. "Wonder what he could have died of?"

In the middle of the burro's neck, as resplendent as the day, the enormous gunshot wound shouted the truth to the sun.

"Who knows? Poison, I guess," a calm Orgaz replied, his hands still buried in his pockets.

But the burros disappeared forever from Orgaz's fenced fields.

During his first years as chief of the Bureau of Records, all San Ignacio protested against Orgaz, who had vigorously set aside all the traditional arrangements and installed his office a half-league from the town. In a small dirt-floored room, darkened by the gallery and by a great mandarin orange tree that almost blocked the doorway, his clients inevitably had to wait for Orgaz, since he was never there—or else he would come in with his hands covered with the black material he used to repair his roof. There the recorder would note down the information as quickly as possible on any old scrap of paper and leave the office before his client, to climb back on his roof.

Actually, this roof was Orgaz's principal occupation during his first four years in Misiones. In Misiones it rains—I'm here to tell it—hard enough to put two layers of zinc to the test. And Orgaz had constructed *his* roof with shingles soaked by the rains of a long autumn. Orgaz's plantings were literally stretching toward the sky, but his roof shingles, too—submitted to the effects of sun and humidity—curled upward at their outer edges, giving the sea-urchin effect we've mentioned.

Seen from below, from within the dark rooms, the dark wood roof had the unusual effect of being the lightest part of the room, since each curled-up shingle acted as a skylight. The shingles, furthermore, were covered with countless daubs of red lead, a packing that Orgaz had applied between the cracks with a hollow length of bamboo where the water poured, not dripped, onto his bed. But the strangest sight was the lengths of cord that Orgaz had used to caulk his roof, which now, hanging loose and weighted with pitch, hung motionless like snakes, reflecting slivers of light.

Orgaz had tried everything he could think of to mend his roof. He tried wedges of wood, plaster, Portland cement, dichromate glue, and pitch and sawdust. After two years of calculations in which he never achieved, as had his most remote ancestors, the pleasure of finding himself sheltered by night from the rain, Orgaz concentrated his attention on the element burlap/bleck. This was a true discovery, and our hero then replaced all the ignoble patches of Portland cement and pressed sawdust with his black cement.

Anyone coming to the office or passing by in the direction of the new port was sure to see the recorder on his roof. After every repair, Orgaz would await a new rain and, without many illusions, go inside to observe its efficacy. The old skylights would hold up rather well, but new cracks would open that dripped—naturally—on the spot where Orgaz had just placed his bed.

And in this eternal struggle between poverty of recourse and a man who wanted above everything else to achieve man's oldest ideal—a roof that would harbor him against rain—Orgaz was surprised where most he had sinned.

Orgaz's office hours were seven to eleven in the morning. We have already seen how, in general, he attended to his duties. When the recorder of the Bureau of Records was in the bush or working in his cassava plantings, the boy summoned him by starting the turbine of the ant-killing machine. Orgaz would come up the hill with his hoe on his shoulder or his machete in his hand, wishing with all his soul that it was one minute past eleven. One

second past the hour, there was no way to force the recorder to
attend to the problems of his office.

On one of these occasions, as Orgaz was climbing down from
the bungalow roof, the cowbell on the front gate rang. Orgaz
glanced at the clock: it was five after eleven. Consequently, he
went calmly to wash his hands in the basin on the big whetstone,
paying no attention to the boy, who was saying to him, "There's
a man here, Patrón."

"Tell him to come tomorrow."

"I told him, but he says he's the inspector from the Department of Justice. . . ."

"That's different; tell him to wait a minute," Orgaz replied.
And he continued to rub grease on his bleck-covered forearms,
while the frown deepened on his forehead.

In fact, he had reason enough to frown.

Orgaz had solicited the positions of justice of the peace and of
recorder in order to make a living. He had no love for his duties,
although he administered justice—sitting on one corner of the
table with a wrench in his hands—with perfect equity. But the
Bureau of Records was his nightmare. Every day he was supposed to enter in the books, and in *duplicate*, all records of births,
deaths, and marriages. Half the time he was called from his tasks
in the field by the turbine, and the other half he was interrupted
in the act of studying, on his roof, some cement that was finally
going to afford him a dry bed. So he would hurriedly note down
this demographic information on the first piece of paper he found
and then flee the office.

Then there was the endless problem of calling witnesses to sign
documents, since every peon would offer as his witness some
weird person who had never been out of the bush. These were
some of the vexations that Orgaz had somehow resolved his first
year but which had tired him once and for all of his duties.

"We're caught out," he said to himself as he finished removing
the bleck from his arms and, out of habit, cast about for an idea.
"If I get out of this, I'll be lucky. . . ."

He went finally to his dark office where the inspector, with great interest, was observing the disorderly table, the two chairs, the earthen floor, and a sock hanging from the roof poles that had been carried there by the rats.

The man knew who Orgaz was, and for a while the two chatted about things foreign to the office. But when the inspector coldly began to discuss the question of duties, it was a very different matter.

In those days the record books were kept in the local offices, where once a year they were inspected. At least, that's what was supposed to be done. But, in practice, sometimes years passed without an inspection—as many as four, in the case of Orgaz. So the inspector was faced with twenty-four books of the Bureau of Records, twelve of which were still unsigned, and twelve of which were totally blank.

The inspector slowly leafed through book after book, never looking up from his inspection. Orgaz, sitting on the corner of the table, was silent. The visitor did not exempt a single page; one by one he slowly turned the blank pages. There was no sign of life in the room—although the room was charged with purpose—except the persistent swinging of Orgaz's boot.

"Well," the inspector said, finally, "Where are the documents relating to these twelve empty books?"

Half turning, Orgaz picked up a biscuit tin and, without a word, emptied it, covering the table with scraps of paper of every kind and appearance—particularly a rough paper still bearing traces of Orgaz's herbariums. Those little pieces of paper—covered with grease pencil, yellow, blue, red, used to mark wood in the bush—created an artistic effect that the inspector considered for a long moment. And then for another moment he looked at Orgaz.

"Well!" he exclaimed. "This is the first time I've seen books like these. Two entire years of unsigned records. And the rest in a biscuit tin. There's only one thing for me to do."

But because of the signs of hard labor on Orgaz's work-roughened hands, he relented a little.

"You're really something!" he said. "You've not even taken the trouble to change the age of your two witnesses every year.

151

You've given it the same in all four years and all twenty-four record books. One witness is always twenty-four and the other thirty-six. And this mess of papers. . . . You are a state official. The state pays you to carry out your duties. Isn't that true?"

"That's true," Orgaz replied.

"Well. For even the hundredth part of this, you should be removed from office this very day. But I don't want to take action. I will give you three days." He added, looking at his watch, "Three days from now I will be in Posadas and will board my boat for the night at eleven. I'll give you until ten o'clock Saturday night to bring me the books, *in order*. If not, I'll take action. Understood?"

"Perfectly," Orgaz answered.

And he accompanied his visitor to the gate, who then waved brusquely and galloped away.

Orgaz slowly walked back over volcanic gravel, which rolled beneath his feet. Black, blacker than the patches on his roof, was the task that awaited him. He made mental calculations: so many minutes for each record—the time it would take to save his position and with it the freedom to continue his "hydrofugic" experiments. Orgaz's only resources were those purveyed by the state for keeping the Bureau of Records books up to date. He had, then, to regain the good will of the state. . . . His position was dangling by a fine thread.

Consequently, Orgaz finished removing the pitch from his hands and sat down at his table to fill in the twelve large books of the Bureau of Records. Alone, he would never have completed his task in the allotted time, but his boy helped him, dictating the information to him.

His helper was a twelve-year-old Polish boy, red-haired, his skin orange with freckles. His eyelashes were so blond they were invisible, even in profile, and he always wore his cap pulled down to his nose because the light hurt his eyes. He lent his services to Orgaz and cooked the food they ate together beneath the mandarin orange tree.

But during those three days the assay kiln the young Pole used for cooking was idle. The boy's mother was commissioned to bring baked cassava to the plateau every morning.

Face to face in the barbecue-hot dark office, Orgaz and his secretary worked without rising, the chief naked to the waist and his assistant with his cap pulled over his eyes, even in the dark interior. For three days the only sounds heard were the singsong schoolboy chant of the young Pole, echoed by Orgaz's bass repeating the last words of each phrase. From time to time they ate a biscuit or some cassava as they continued their task. They worked this way till late afternoon. And when Orgaz would drag himself past the bamboos to bathe, his weary body spoke very clearly of his fatigue.

The north wind blew mercilessly those three days, and the air vibrated with heat on the office roof. That little corner of earth, nevertheless, was the only shaded area on the plateau, and from the office the scribes could see, through the branches of the orange tree, a shimmering square of sand that seemed to hum through the entire siesta time.

After Orgaz's bath, the task would begin anew. They carried the table outside into the quiet and suffocating atmosphere. Among the rigid palms of the plateau, so black they stood out even against the shadows, the scribes continued to fill in the pages of the Bureau of Records by the light of a lantern among a nimbus of small multicolored satin butterflies that swarmed around the base of the lantern and settled in throngs upon the white pages. This made the task more difficult, for if these butterflies, dressed for a ball, are the most beautiful that Misiones can offer on an asphyxiatingly hot night, nothing is more tenacious than the advance of these silken ladies against the pen of a man no longer strong enough to hold a pen—or let it go.

Orgaz slept four hours during the last two days, and on the last night, alone on the plateau with his palm trees, his lantern, and his butterflies, he did not sleep at all. The sky was so heavy and so low that he could feel it pressing against his forehead. In the early hours, however, he thought he heard through the silence a deep and distant sound—the drumming of rain on leaves. That afternoon, in fact, the horizon had been very dark in the southwest.

"Just so the Yabebirí doesn't act up . . . ," he said to himself, peering through the shadows.

The dawn came at last; the sun came out; and Orgaz returned to the office with his lantern, which he left hanging in a corner, forgotten, illuminating the floor. Alone, he continued writing. And when at ten o'clock the young Pole finally awakened from his fatigue, he still had time to help his *patrón*, who at two o'clock in the afternoon, his face grimy and dirty, threw down his pen and literally collapsed upon his arms, where he remained for so long one could not see his breathing.

He had finished. After sixty-three hours, hour after hour, facing the square of burning white sand on the lugubrious plateau, his twenty-four Bureau of Records books were in order. But he had missed the launch that left at one for Posadas. There was no recourse but to ride there on horseback.

As he was saddling his horse, Orgaz observed the weather. The sky was white, and the sun, although veiled by vapors, burned like fire. From the tiered mountains of Paraguay, from the fluvial basin in the southeast came an impression of dampness, of damp hot jungle. But while all around the horizon stripes of livid water streaked the sky, San Ignacio was still choking in oven-dry heat.

Under such conditions, then, Orgaz trotted and galloped as fast as possible in the direction of Posadas. He descended the hill of the new cemetery and entered the valley of the Yabebirí. He had his first surprise when he saw the river; as he was waiting for the raft, a border of little sticks was bubbling against the shore.

"It's rising," the man on the raft said to the traveler. "It poured today and last night upstream. . . ."

"And down below?" Orgaz asked.

"There, too."

Orgaz had not been mistaken, then, when the night before he thought he had heard the drumming of rain on the distant forest.

Uneasy now about crossing the Garupá, whose sudden floods can only be compared to those of the Yabebirí, Orgaz ascended the slopes of Loreto at a gallop, damaging his horse's hoofs on the basalt stones. From the high plains that stretched before his view into an enormous landscape, he saw the whole span of the sky, from the east to the south, heavy with blue water, and the forest, drowned in rain, dimly visible through white mists. There was no sun now, and a barely perceptible breeze occasionally infiltrated the asphyxiating calm. He sensed contact with water—the deluge following the long droughts. And galloping swiftly, passing through Santa Ana, Orgaz reached Candelaria.

There he met his second—although anticipated—surprise: the Garupá, flowing swollen from four days of bad weather, forbade crossing. No ford, no raft; only fermented refuse bobbing amidst pieces of straw, and, in the channel, sticks and water rushing full speed.

What to do? It was five o'clock. Another five hours and the inspector would be going on board to sleep. Orgaz's only choice was to reach the Paraná and get into the first craft he found along the shore.

That was what he did; and, as it began to grow dark beneath the most menacing storm ever seen in any sky, Orgaz descended the Paraná in a stove-in boat mended with a piece of tin that had holes through which water poured in streams like cat's whiskers.

For a while the owner of the boat poled lazily down the middle of the river, but, as he was filled with rum acquired with Orgaz's advance payment, he soon preferred at the least excuse to philosophize with first one and then the other shore. At this juncture Orgaz took command of an oar at the same time that a brusque blast of cool, almost wintry, wind stirred the river into little peaks like those on a grater. Rains came that obscured the Argentine coast. And with the first enormous drops, Orgaz thought about his books, barely sheltered by the cloth of his case. He took off his jacket and shirt, covered the books with them, and again took the oar at the prow. The Indian worked, too, uneasy in the storm. And beneath the riddling deluge those two individuals held the boat in the channel, paddling vigorously, their view limited to only twenty meters, enclosed in a circle of white.

Their keeping in the main channel was conducive to speed, and Orgaz held them to it as much as possible. But the wind rose, and the Paraná, which spreads as wide as a sea between Candelaria and Posadas, curled into great mad waves. Orgaz had sat upon his books to save them from the water breaking against, and occasionally flooding into, the boat. He could not, nevertheless, continue indefinitely, and even though it meant arriving late in Posadas, he headed toward the shore. And if the waterlogged boat battered from the sides by large waves did not sink in the crossing, it was only because inexplicable things happen sometimes.

The rain continued, closing them in. The two men, streaming water, looking somehow thinner, got out of the boat, and as they climbed the barranca they saw a dark shadow looming before them. Orgaz's brow cleared, and, overjoyed that his books would be miraculously saved, he ran to take shelter there.

He found himself in an old shed used for drying bricks. Orgaz sat down on a stone amidst the wood ashes, while at the very entrance, squatting with his face between his hands, the Indian tranquilly awaited the end of the rain that was drumming on the zinc roof with a rhythm that increased by the minute to a dizzying roar.

Orgaz, too, looked outside. What an interminable day! He felt it had been a month since he had left San Ignacio. The Yabebirí rising . . . the baked cassava . . . the night he had spent alone, writing . . . staring at the patch of burning sand for twelve hours. . . .

Far away . . . , all that seemed so far away. He was soaked, and his body ached abominably, but this was nothing compared to how sleepy he was. If only he could sleep, sleep . . . , if only for an instant. But he couldn't, as much as he wanted to, for the ashes were alive with chiggers. Orgaz emptied the water from his boots, put them on again, and went out to look at the weather.

Abruptly, the rain had ceased. The crepuscular calm was choking with humidity, and Orgaz was not deceived by the ephemeral truce that would resolve into a new deluge as night approached. But he decided to take advantage of the respite, and he set out on foot.

He calculated the distance to Posadas at six or seven kilometers. In normal weather, that would have been an easy trip, but the boots of an exhausted man slip in heavy clay and gain no ground, and Orgaz completed those seven kilometers in darkest shadows from the waist down, his body from the waist up glowing in the haze from the electric lights of Posadas.

Suffering, the torment of his need for sleep buzzing in a head that seemed split open in several places, beyond exhaustion, these things were more than enough to defeat him. But Orgaz's dominant emotion was that of self-satisfaction. The satisfaction of having rehabilitated himself stood out above everything else— this is how he would appear to the inspector from the Department of Justice. Orgaz had not been born to be a public official; he really *wasn't* a public official, as we have seen. But he felt in his heart the sweet warmth that comforts a man when he has worked hard to fulfill a simple task, and he pressed forward, quarter-mile after quarter-mile, until he saw a blinding light, not reflected in the sky now, but the lamps themselves . . . Posadas.

The hotel clock was striking ten when the inspector, closing his valise, saw standing before him a pale man, mud covered from head to toe, with obvious signs of falling should he let go of the frame of the door.

For the moment, the inspector stood mutely staring at this apparition. When the man managed to take a step forward and place his books upon the table, he recognized Orgaz, although he was still puzzled by his presence there in such a state and at such an hour.

"And what is this?" he asked, pointing to the books.

"As you requested," Orgaz said. "In order."

The inspector looked at Orgaz, considered his appearance a moment, and then, remembering the incident in Orgaz's office, began to laugh in a friendly way as he slapped Orgaz on the back.

"But I told you that just to have something to say! You've been a fool, man! Why did you go to all that trouble?"

One burning midday when we were with Orgaz on his roof—he inserting heavy rolls of pitch and bleck between the wooden shingles—he told me this story.

He made no comment at all as he finished. Nine years have passed since that incident took place; I do not know what the pages of his record books held in that moment or what there was in his biscuit tin. But I wouldn't for anything in the world have wanted to be the inspector who deprived Orgaz of the satisfaction he had won that night.

The Son

It is a powerful summer day in Misiones, with all the sun, heat, and calm the season can offer. Nature, at its fullest and most open, seems satisfied with itself.

Like the sun, the heat, and the calm surroundings, the father, too, opens his heart to nature.

"Be careful, little one," he says to his son, summing up all his warnings for the occasion in the one phrase, which his son fully understands.

"Yes, *papá*," responds the child as he picks up the shotgun, fills his shirt pockets with shells, and then carefully buttons the pockets.

"Come back by noon," his father says.

"Yes, *papá*," the young boy repeats.

Balancing the shotgun in his hand, he smiles at his father, kisses him, and leaves.

The father follows him for a moment with his eyes and then returns to his day's tasks, made happy by his young one's joy.

He knows that his son, raised from tender infancy to be cautious in the presence of danger, can handle a firearm and hunt anything that presents itself. Although very tall for his age, he is only thirteen. And he might seem even younger if one were to judge by the purity of his blue eyes, still fresh with childish surprise.

The father doesn't have to raise his eyes from his task to follow in his mind the son's progress. Now, he has crossed the red path and is heading straight for the woods through the opening in the esparto grass.

He knows that hunting in the woods—hunting game—requires more patience than his son can muster. After cutting through the woods his cub will skirt the line of cactus and go to the marsh in search of doves, toucans, or perhaps a pair of herons like the one his friend Juan sighted several days ago.

Only now, a ghost of a smile touches the father's lips as he recalls the two young boys' love of hunting. Sometimes they get only a *yacútoro*, even less frequently a *surucuá*, and, even so, return in triumph, Juan to his own ranch with the nine-gauge shotgun that he himself has given him, and his son to their mesa with the huge sixteen-gauge Saint-Etienne—a white powder, four-lock shotgun.

The father had been exactly the same. At thirteen he would have given his life for a shotgun. Now at that age his son has one—and the father smiles.

It isn't easy, nevertheless, for a widowed father, whose only hope and faith lies in the life of his son, to raise the boy as he has, free within his limited range of action, sure of hand and foot since he was four years old, conscious of the immensity of certain dangers and the limitations of his own strength.

The father has had to battle fiercely against what he considers his own selfishness. So easy for a child to miscalculate, to place a foot in empty space, and . . . one loses a son! Danger always exists for man at any age, but its threat is lessened if, from the time one is a child, he is accustomed to rely on nothing but his own strength.

This is the way the father has raised his son. And to achieve it he has had to resist his heart as well as his moral torments, because this father, a man with a weak stomach and poor sight, has suffered for some time from hallucinations.

He has seen visions of a former happiness—embodied in most painful illusions—that should have remained forever buried in the oblivion in which he has shut himself. He has not escaped the torment of visions concerning his own son. He has *seen* him hammering a *parabellum* bullet on the shop forge, *seen* him fall to the ground covered in blood—when what the boy was really doing was polishing the buckle of his hunting belt.

Horrible things. . . . But today, this burning, vital summer day, the love of which the son seems to have inherited, the father

162

feels happy, tranquil, and sure of the future.

In that instant, not far away, a sharp crack sounds.

"The Saint-Etienne," the father thinks, recognizing the detonation. "Two fewer doves in the woods. . . ." Paying no further attention to the insignificant event, the man once again loses himself in his task.

The sun, already very high, continues to rise. Everywhere one looks—rocks, land, trees—the air, as rarefied as if in an oven, vibrates with heat. A deep humming sound fills the soul and saturates the surrounding countryside as far as the eye can see— at this hour the essence of all tropical life.

The father glances at his wrist: twelve o'clock. And he raises his eyes to the woods.

His son should be on his way back now. They never betray the confidence each has in the other—the silver-haired father and the thirteen-year-old boy. When his son responds, "Yes, *papá*," he will do what he says. He had said he would be back before twelve, and the father had smiled as he watched him set off.

But the son has not returned.

The man returns to his chores, forcing himself to concentrate on his task. It is easy, so easy, to lose track of time in the woods, to sit on the ground for a while, resting, not moving. . . .

Suddenly the noonday light, the tropical hum, and the father's heart skip a beat at the thought he has just had: his son resting, not moving. . . .

Time has gone by: it is 12:30. The father steps out of his workshop, and, as he rests his hand on the mechanic's bench, the explosion of a *parabellum* bullet surges from the depths of his memory; and instantly, for the first time in three hours, he realizes he has heard nothing since the blast from the Saint-Etienne. He has not heard stones turning under a familiar step. His son has not returned, and all nature stands arrested at the edge of the woods, awaiting him. . . .

Ah! A temperate character and blind confidence in the upbringing of a son are not sufficient to frighten away the specter of calamity that a weak-sighted father sees rising from the edge of

163

the woods. Distraction, forgetfulness, an unexpected delay: his heart cannot accept any of these reasons; none would delay his son's return.

One shot, one single shot, has sounded, and that a long time ago. The father has heard no sound since, has seen no bird; not one single person has come out of the opening in the esparto grass to tell him that at a wire fence . . . a great disaster. . . .

Without his machete, distracted, the father sets out. He cuts through the opening in the grass, enters the woods, skirts the line of cactus—without finding the least trace of his son.

All nature seems to stand still. And after the father has traveled the well-known hunting paths and explored the marsh in vain, he knows surely that each step forward carries him, fatally and inexorably, toward the body of his son.

Nothing even to reproach himself for, poor creature. Only the cold, terrible, and final realization: his son has killed himself going over a . . .

But where . . . where! There are so many wire fences and the woods are so foul. Oh, so very foul . . . ! If one is not careful crossing a fence with a shotgun in his hand . . .

The father stifles a shout. He has seen something rising. . . . No, it isn't his son, no . . . ! And he turns in a different direction, and then another and another. . . .

Nothing would be gained here by showing the pallor of the man's skin or the anguish in his eyes. The man still has not called his son. Although his heart clamors for him, his mouth remains mute. He is sure that the mere act of pronouncing his son's name, of calling him aloud, will be the confession of his death.

"Boy!" escapes from him abruptly. . . .

No one, nothing, responds. The father, who has aged ten years, walks down the sun-reddened paths searching for the son who has just died.

"Sonny! My little boy!" The diminutive rises from the depths of his soul.

Once before, in the midst of happiness and peace, this father had suffered the hallucination of seeing his son rolling on the ground, his forehead pierced by a bullet. Now, in every dark corner of the woods he sees sparkling wire; and at the foot of a fence post, his discharged shotgun at his side, he sees . . .

"Son! My little boy!"

Even the forces that submit a poor hallucinated father to the most atrocious nightmares have their limits. And our father feels his reason slipping away—when suddenly he sees his son step out of a cross path.

The look on the face of a father in the woods without his machete is enough to cause a thirteen-year-old boy to hasten his step, his eyes moist.

"My little boy," the man murmurs and drops exhausted to the white sand, clasping his arms about his son's legs.

The child stands, his legs encircled, and, as he understands his father's pain, slowly caresses his head, "Poor *papá*. . . ."

Time begins again. Soon it will be three o'clock. Together now, father and son undertake the return home; and if one can admit to tears in the voice of a strong man, let us mercifully close our ears to the anguish crying in that voice.

"Why didn't you watch the sun to keep track of the time?" the father murmurs.

"I looked, *papá*. . . . But as I started back I saw Juan's herons and I followed them. . . ."

"What you have put me through, my son . . . !"

"Pah-pah . . . ," the boy murmurs, too.

After a long silence: "And the herons, did you kill them?" the father asks.

"No. . . ."

An unimportant detail, after all. Under the blazing sky, in the open, cutting through the esparto, the man returns home with his son, his arm resting happily on the boy's shoulders, almost as high as his own. He returns bathed in sweat, and, though broken in body and soul, he smiles with happiness. . . .

He smiles with hallucinated happiness. . . . Because this father walks alone. He has found no one, and his arm is resting upon empty air. Because behind him, at the foot of a fence post, with his legs higher than his body, caught in a wire fence, his beloved son, dead since ten o'clock in the morning, lies in the sun.